TEA TIME FOR THE TRADITIONALLY BUILT

Alexander McCall Smith

WINDSOR
PARAGON

First published 2009
by Little, Brown
This Large Print edition published 2009
by BBC Audiobooks Ltd
by arrangement with
Little, Brown Book Group

Hardcover ISBN: 978 1 408 42931 0
Softcover   ISBN: 978 1 408 42932 7

British Library Cataloguing in Publication Data available

Printed and bound in Great Britain by
CPI Antony Rowe, Chippenham and Eastbourne

TEA TIME FOR THE TRADITIONALLY BUILT

For Iain and Alison Bruce

CHAPTER ONE

MR MOLOFOLOLO

Traditionally built people may not look as if they are great walkers, but there was a time when Precious Ramotswe walked four miles a day. As a girl in Mochudi, all those years ago, a pupil at the school that looked down over the sprawling village below, she went to her lessons every morning on foot, joining the trickle of children that made its way up the hill, the girls in blue tunics, the boys in khaki shirts and shorts, like little soldiers. The journey from the house where she lived with her father and the older cousin who looked after her took all of an hour, except, of course, when she was lucky and managed to ride on the mule-drawn water cart that occasionally passed that way. The driver of this cart, with whom her father had worked in the gold mines as a young man, knew who she was and always slowed down to allow her to clamber up on the driver's seat beside him.

Other children would watch enviously, and try to wave down the water cart. 'I cannot carry all Botswana,' said the driver. 'If I gave all you children a ride on my cart, then my poor mules would die. Their hearts would burst. I cannot allow that.'

'But you have Precious up there!' called out the boys. 'Why is she so special?'

The driver looked at Precious and winked. 'Tell them why you are special, Precious. Explain it to them.'

1

The young Mma Ramotswe, barely eight, was overwhelmed by embarrassment.

'But I am not special. I am just a girl.'

'You are the daughter of Obed Ramotswe,' said the driver. 'He is a great man. That is why you are riding up here.'

He was right, of course—at least in what he said about Obed Ramotswe, who was, by any standards, a fine man. At that age, Precious had only a faint inkling of what her father stood for; later on, as a young woman, she would come to understand what it was to be the daughter of Obed Ramotswe. But in those days, on the way to school, whether riding in state on the water cart or walking along the side of that dusty road with her friends, she had school to think about, with its lessons on so many subjects—the history of Botswana, from the beginning, when it was known as Khama's country, across the plains of which great lions walked, to the emergence of the new Botswana, then still a chrysalis in a dangerous world; writing lessons, with the letters of the alphabet being described in white chalk on an ancient blackboard, all whirls and loops; arithmetic, with its puzzling multiplication tables that needed to be learned by heart—when there was so much else that the heart had to learn.

The water cart, of course, did not pass very often, and so on most days there was a long trudge to school and a long walk back. Some children had an even greater journey; in one class there was a boy who walked seven miles there and seven miles back, even in the hottest of months, when the sun came down upon Botswana like a pounding fist, when the cattle huddled together under the

2

umbrella shade of the acacia trees, not daring to wander off in search of what scraps of grass remained. This boy thought nothing of his daily journey; this is what you did if you wanted to go to school to learn the things that your parents had never had the chance to learn. And you did not complain, even if during the rainy season you might narrowly escape being struck by lightning or being washed away by the torrents that rose in the previously dry watercourses. You did not complain in that Botswana.

Now, of course, it was different, and it was the contemplation of these differences that made Mma Ramotswe think about walking again.

'We are becoming lazy, Mma Ramotswe,' said Mma Makutsi one afternoon, as they sipped their afternoon cup of redbush tea in the offices of the No. 1 Ladies' Detective Agency. 'Have you noticed? We are becoming lazy.'

Mma Ramotswe frowned. There were times when Mma Makutsi made statements that suffered from that classic flaw of all generalisations—they were just too general. This observation, it seemed to her, could be such a remark.

'Do you mean that you and I are becoming lazy?' she asked her assistant. 'If you do, then I do not think that's right, Mma Makutsi. Take this morning, for instance. We finished that report on security at the loan office. And we wrote a lot of letters. Six, seven, I think. That is not being lazy.'

Mma Makutsi raised a hand in protest. 'No, Mma, I did not mean that. I did not mean to say that you and I are becoming lazy. Or not specially lazy. I am talking about everybody.'

Mma Ramotswe raised an eyebrow. 'The whole

3

of Botswana?'

Mma Makutsi nodded. 'Yes, the whole country. And it's not just Botswana, Mma. We are no worse than anybody else. In fact, I am sure that there are many much lazier countries elsewhere. What I really meant was that people in general are becoming lazy.'

Mma Ramotswe, who had been prepared to defend Botswana against Mma Makutsi's accusations, relaxed. If the remark was about people in general, and not just about the residents of Gaborone, then Mma Makutsi's theory could at least be heard out. 'Why do you say that people are becoming lazy, Mma?' she asked.

Mma Makutsi glanced through the half-open door that led from the agency into the garage. On the other side of the workshop, Mr J. L. B. Matekoni was showing his two apprentices an engine part. 'You see those two boys out there?' she said. 'Charlie and . . .'

'Fanwell,' supplied Mma Ramotswe. 'We must start using his name. It is not kind to be forgetting it all the time.'

'Yes, Charlie and . . . Fanwell,' said Mma Makutsi. 'It is a stupid name, though, don't you think, Mma? Why would anybody be called Fanwell?'

Mma Ramotswe could not let this pass. Mma Makutsi was too hard on the two apprentices, particularly on the older one, Charlie. Words had passed between them more than once, including on the occasion when Charlie had called Mma Makutsi a warthog and made disparaging references to her large glasses. It had been quite wrong of him, and Mma Ramotswe had made that plain, but she had also acknowledged that he had been provoked. 'They are young men,' she had said to Mma Makutsi. 'That is what young men are like, Mma. Their heads are full of loud music and thoughts of girls. Imagine walking around with all that nonsense in your head.'

That had been said in defence of Charlie; now it was necessary to say something for Fanwell. It was wrong of Mma Makutsi, she thought, to poke fun at Fanwell's name. 'Why is anybody called anything, Mma Makutsi? That boy cannot help it. It is the parents who give children stupid names. It is the fault of the parents.'

'But Fanwell, Mma Ramotswe? What a silly name. Why did they not call him Fanbelt? That would be a good name for an apprentice mechanic, wouldn't it? Hah! Fanbelt. That would be very funny.'

'No, Mma Makutsi,' said Mma Ramotswe. 'We must not make fun of people's names. There are some who think that your own name, Grace, is a strange name. I do not think that, of course. But there are probably people like that.'

Mma Makutsi was dismissive. 'Then they are very foolish,' she said. 'They should know better.'

'And that is what Fanwell himself would probably say about anybody who laughed at his name,' Mma Ramotswe pointed out.

Mma Makutsi had to agree with this, even if reluctantly. She and Mma Ramotswe were fortunate, with their reasonably straightforward names of Grace and Precious respectively; she had contemporaries who were not so fortunate and had been saddled by their parents with names that were frankly ridiculous. One boy she had known at

5

school had borne a Setswana name which meant *Look out, the police have arrived*. The poor boy had been the object of derision amongst his classmates and had tried, unsuccessfully, to change the name by which he was known. But names, like false allegations, stick, and he had gone through life with this unfortunate burden, reminded of it every time he had to give details for an official form; looking away so that the person examining the form could be given the opportunity to smile, which they all did.

'Even if their names are not their fault,' said Mma Makutsi, 'the way those boys behave *is* their fault, Mma. There can be no doubt about that. And those boys are very lazy, Mma. They are examples of what I am talking about.'

She looked sternly at Mma Ramotswe, as if challenging her employer to contradict her. Mma Ramotswe did not rise to the bait; Mma Makutsi was rather assertive—and she admired the younger woman for that—but it did not help, she had decided, to engage with her too much when she was in mid-theory. It was best to let people have their say, she always felt; then, when they had finished, and had possibly run out of breath, one could always lodge a mild objection to what had been said before.

Mma Makutsi peered in the direction of the garage, and lowered her voice. 'Have you ever seen those two young men walking?' she asked.

Mma Ramotswe frowned. Of course she had seen the apprentices walking; they walked about the garage, they came into the office to collect their tea, they walked to the tree under which Mr J. L. B. Matekoni's truck was parked. She pointed this out to Mma Makutsi, gently enough, but not so mildly as to prevent a firm refutation from the other side of the room.

'Not that sort of walking, Mma,' said Mma Makutsi. 'Anybody can walk across a room or round a garage. Anybody, Mma. Even those two lazy young men. The sort of walking I'm talking about is walking from one place to another. Walking to work. Walking from the middle of town to the National Stadium. Walking from Kgale Siding to Gaborone. That sort of walking.'

'Those are not short walks,' said Mma Ramotswe. 'Although it would not take too long, I think, to get from the middle of town to the Stadium. Perhaps twenty-five minutes if it was not too hot.'

Mma Makutsi sniffed. 'How can we tell?' she asked. 'These days nobody would know how long it takes to walk anywhere because we have all stopped walking, Mma. We know how long it takes to drive. We know how long a minibus takes. But we do not know how long it takes to walk.'

Mma Ramotswe was silent as she thought about this. She had long understood that one of the features of Mma Makutsi's speeches was that there was often a grain of truth in them, and sometimes even more than that.

'And here's another thing, Mma Ramotswe,' Mma Makutsi continued. 'Have you heard of evolution? Well, what will happen if we all carry on being lazy like this and drive everywhere? I can tell you, Mma. We shall start to grow wheels. That is what evolution is all about.'

Mma Ramotswe laughed. 'Surely not, Mma!'

But Mma Makutsi was serious. 'Oh yes,

Mma Ramotswe. Our fingers have evolved so that we can do things like typing. That is well known. Why should our legs not evolve in the same way? They will become circular, I think, and they will turn round and round. That is what will happen, Mma, if we are not careful.'

Mma Ramotswe could not keep herself from smiling. 'I do not think that will happen, Mma.'

Mma Makutsi pursed her lips. 'We shall see, Mma.'

Mma Ramotswe almost said: *But we shall not, Mma Makutsi, because evolution takes a long time, and you and I shall not be around to see the results.* But she did not, because Mma Makutsi's remarks had struck a chord within her and she wanted to think about them a bit more. When had she herself last walked any distance at all? It was sobering to realise that she could not remember. She usually went for a walk around her garden shortly after dawn—and sometimes in the evenings as well—but that was not very far, and she often spent more time looking at plants, or standing and thinking, than walking. And for the rest, she used her tiny white van, driving in it each morning to the No. 1 Ladies' Detective Agency and then driving home again at the end of the day. And if she went to the shops at River Walk, to the supermarket where there had been that dramatic chase with shopping carts, she drove there too, parking as close to the entrance as she could, so that she did not have a long walk across the car park. No, she was as good an example as anybody of what Mma Makutsi had been talking about. And so was Mma Potokwani, the matron of the orphan farm, who drove everywhere in that old van that they used to

8

transport the children; and Mr J. L. B. Matekoni, too, who was even more implicated in this epidemic of laziness, given that he fixed cars and vans and thereby enabled people to avoid walking.

No, Mma Makutsi was right, or, even if she was not entirely right, was a bit right. Cars had changed Botswana; cars had changed everywhere, and Mma Ramotswe was not at all sure that this change was entirely for the better.

I shall start walking a bit more, she resolved. It is not enough just to identify a problem; there were plenty of people who were very skilled at pointing out what was wrong with the world, but they were not always so adept at working out how these things could be righted. Mma Ramotswe did not wish to be one of these armchair critics; she would do something. She would start walking to work on . . . she almost decided on three days of each week, but then thought that two days would be quite enough. And she would start tomorrow.

On the way home that evening, the idea of walking came back to Mma Ramotswe. The idea returned, though, not because she remembered what Mma Makutsi had said about laziness, but because the tiny white van, which in the past few months had intermittently been making a strange noise, was now making that noise again, but louder than before. It happened as she made her way into Zebra Drive; turning a corner always put a strain on the tiny white van, which was something do with the suspension and what Mr J. L. B. Matekoni referred to politely as the 'distribution of load'. Mma Ramotswe had pondered this expression and then asked, perhaps rather bluntly, 'And the load, I take it, Mr J. L. B. Matekoni, is me?'

He had looked away to cover his embarrassment. 'You could say that, Mma Ramotswe. But then all of us are loads when it comes to vehicles. Even one of these very thin model ladies will be a load . . .' He trailed off. He was not making it any better, he thought, and Mma Ramotswe was looking at him in an expectant way.

When it became apparent that he had nothing further to add, Mma Ramotswe had continued, 'Yes, Mr J. L. B. Matekoni, there are such ladies. And unfortunately they are becoming more common. There are now many of them.' She paused. 'But perhaps they will begin to disappear. They will get thinner and thinner, and more and more fashionable, and then . . . pouf . . . they will be blown away by the wind.'

This remark reduced the tension that had built, and they both laughed. 'That will teach them,' he said. 'They will be blown away while the other ladies will still be here because the wind will not be strong enough to lift . . .' He stopped once more; Mma Ramotswe was again looking at him expectantly.

The distribution of load, that evidently led to difficulties, but now, as the van started to make an alarming sound again, she realised that this had nothing to do with suspension and traditionally built drivers. This had to do with some fundamental sickness deep in the engine itself; the tiny white van was sick at heart.

She lifted her foot off the accelerator to see if that would help, but all that it did was to reduce the volume of the knocking sound. And when she put her foot down on the pedal again, the noise resumed. Only at a very slow speed, barely above walking pace, did the sound disappear altogether. It was as if the van was saying to her: *I am old now; I can still move, but I must move at the pace of a very old van.*

She continued her progress down Zebra Drive, steering the van carefully through her gateway with all the care of a nurse wheeling a very sick patient down the corridor of a hospital. Then she parked the van under its habitual tree at the side of the house and climbed out of the driving seat. As she went inside, she debated with herself what to do. She was married to a mechanic, a situation in which any woman would revel, especially when her car broke down. Mechanics made good husbands, as did carpenters and plumbers—that was well known—and any woman proposed to by such a man would do well to accept. But for every advantage that attended any particular man, it always seemed as if there was a compensating disadvantage lurking somewhere. The mechanic as husband could be counted on to get a car going again, but he could just as surely be counted upon to be eager to change the car. Mechanics were very rarely satisfied with what they had, in mechanical terms, that is, and often wanted their customers— or indeed their wives—to change one car for another. If Mma Ramotswe told Mr J. L. B. Matekoni that the tiny white van was making a strange noise, she knew exactly what he would say, as he had said it all before.

'It's time to replace the van, Mma Ramotswe,' he had said, only a few months earlier. And then he had added, 'No vehicle lasts for ever, you know.'

'I know that, Mr J. L. B. Matekoni,' she said.

11

'But surely it's wrong to replace a vehicle that still has a lot of life left in it. That's not very responsible, I think.'

'Your van is over twenty,' he said. 'Twenty-two years old, I believe. That is about half the age of Botswana itself.'

It had not been a wise comparison and Mma Ramotswe seized on it. 'So you would replace Botswana?' she said. 'When a country gets old, you say, *That's enough, let's get a new country.* I'm surprised at you, Mr J. L. B. Matekoni.'

This unsatisfactory conversation had ended there, but Mma Ramotswe knew that if she reported the van to him it would be tantamount to signing its death warrant. She thought about that this evening, as she prepared the potatoes for the family dinner. The house was quiet: Mr J. L. B. Matekoni was not going to be in until later, as he had delivered one car to Lobatse and was coming back in another. The two foster-children, Puso and Motholeli, were in their rooms, tackling their homework, or so Mma Ramotswe thought, until she heard the sound of laughter drifting down the corridor. She imagined that they were sharing a joke, or the memory of something amusing that had happened at school that day, a remark made by a friend, a humiliation suffered by an unpopular teacher.

The laughter suddenly broke out again, and this time it was followed by giggles. Homework had to be finished by dinner-time; that was the rule, and too much laughing at jokes would not help that. Putting down her potato peeler, Mma Ramotswe went to investigate.

'Motholeli?' she asked outside the girl's closed

door.

The giggling that had been going on inside the room stopped abruptly. Tapping lightly—Mma Ramotswe always respected the children's privacy—she pushed the door open.

Motholeli was in her wheelchair near her small work-table, facing another girl of similar age, who was sitting in the chair beside the bed. The two had been giggling uncontrollably, as their eyes, Mma Ramotswe noticed, had tears of laughter in the corners.

'Your homework must be very funny today,' Mma Ramotswe said.

Motholeli glanced conspiratorially at her friend, and then looked back at Mma Ramotswe. 'This is my friend,' she said. 'She is called Alice.'

Mma Ramotswe looked at the other girl, who rose to her feet politely and lowered her head. The greetings exchanged, the visitor sat down.

'Have you done your homework, Motholeli?' Mma Ramotswe asked.

The girl replied that it was completely finished; it had been easy, she said; so simple that even Puso could have done it, and he was several years younger.

'The reason why our homework is so simple today,' Alice explained, 'is that the teacher who gave it to us is not very intelligent. She can only mark simple homework.'

This observation set the two girls giggling again, and Mma Ramotswe had to bite her lip to prevent herself from giggling too. But she could not join in the girls' mirth at the expense of a teacher. Teachers had to be respected—as they always had been in Botswana—and if children thought them stupid, then that would hardly encourage respect.

'I do not think that this teacher can be like that,' said Mma Ramotswe. 'Teachers have to pass examinations. They are very well-educated.'

'Not this one,' said Motholeli, setting the two children off in paroxysms of laughter.

Mma Ramotswe gave up. There was no point in trying to stop teenage girls from giggling; that was the way they were. One might as well try to stop men liking football. The analogy made her stop and think. Football. Tomorrow morning, if she remembered correctly, Mr Leungo Molofololo had arranged to come to see her at ten o'clock. Mma Ramotswe was used to receiving well-known people, but Mr Molofololo, by any standards, would be an important client. Not only did he have a large house up at Phulukane—a house which must have cost many millions of pula to build—but he had the ear of virtually every influential person in the country. Mr Molofololo controlled the country's best football team, and that, in the world of men, counted for more than anything else.

'He is just a man,' Mma Makutsi had said, after Mr Molofololo's secretary had called to make the appointment. 'The fact that he has a football team is neither here nor there, Mma. He is the same as any man.'

But Mma Ramotswe thought differently. Mr Molofololo was not just any man; he was Mr Football.

CHAPTER TWO

WALKING IS GOOD FOR YOU, AND FOR BOTSWANA

The next morning, over breakfast, Mma Ramotswe announced to Mr J. L. B. Matekoni that she would be walking to work that day. She had taken the decision an hour or so earlier, in the middle of her habitual stroll around her garden, shortly after inspecting the pawpaw trees that marked the boundary between her plot and the small piece of wasteland that ran behind it. She had planted the trees herself when first she had come to Zebra Drive and the garden had been nothing, just hard earth, scrub and sour weeds. Now the trees were laden with fruit, heavy yellow orbs that she would shortly pick and enjoy. She liked pawpaw, but neither Mr J. L. B. Matekoni nor the children did, and so these would be for her alone, a private treat, served with orange juice and topped, perhaps, with a small sprinkling of sugar.

Beside the pawpaw trees was an acacia tree in which birds liked to pause on their journeys and in which Mr J. L. B. Matekoni had once seen a long green snake, curled around a branch, its tail hanging down like an elongated twig to be brushed against by some unwary person passing below. The sighting of snakes was an everyday occurrence in Botswana, but the unfortunate creatures were never left alone. Mma Ramotswe did not like to kill them and had thoroughly agreed with a recent public plea from the Wildlife Department that people should refrain from doing anything about snakes unless they actually came into the house. They have their place, said the official, and if there were no snakes then there would be many more rats, and all the rats would make quick work of the patiently gathered harvest.

That message, though, went against most people's deepest instincts. Mma Makutsi, for example, had no time for snakes, and would not hesitate to dispose of one should she have the chance.

'It's all very well for the Government, Mma Ramotswe,' she said. 'Tell me, are there any snakes coming into government offices? These government people do not have to live with snakes as people do in the villages or at the cattle posts. You ask those people out there what to do about snakes and you will get a very different answer.'

She then went on to tell Mma Ramotswe about an incident which she claimed had happened at Bobonong when she was a girl. A large snake—a mamba—had taken up residence in a tree beside a popular path. From one of its branches this snake had dropped down on an old man walking below, with tragic consequences; nobody could survive a mamba bite, least of all an old man. How did Mma Ramotswe think they dealt with the problem?

Mma Ramotswe thought for a moment. 'I think that they probably got one of the women to make up a big pot of hot porridge,' said Mma Ramotswe. 'Boiling hot. That woman put a cloth on her head and balanced the pot of porridge on top of that. Then she walked under the tree and called out to the snake. Mambas think that very rude. So it dropped down into the porridge and was burned. I

16

imagine that is probably what happened, Mma.'

Mma Makutsi stared at her, wide-eyed. 'But that is extraordinary, Mma. That is it exactly. How did you guess?'

Mma Ramotswe smiled, but said nothing. She did not tell Mma Makutsi that this story was an old one, and that she had heard it from one of her aunts, who had presumably heard it from her mother. There were many such stories, and perhaps a long time ago some of them had been true. Now they had acquired the force of truth, innocently enough, and people really believed that these things had happened.

She looked up at her acacia tree. There could be a snake in the tree for all she knew; nature was full of snake-like shapes and colours—long, sinuous twigs and boughs, snake-coloured grass that moved in the wind just as a snake might move. Concealment was easy. So snakes could watch us silently, their tongues flickering in and out to pick up our scent, their tiny, pitch-black eyes bright with evil; they were there, but the best way to deal with snakes was *not* to deal with them—Mma Ramotswe was sure of that. If we left snakes alone, then they kept away from us. It was only when we intruded on their world that they bit us, and who could blame them for that? It was the same with life in general, thought Mma Ramotswe. If we worried away at troublesome issues we often only ended up making things worse. It was far better to let things sort themselves out.

She moved away from the acacia tree and began to make her way slowly back to the house. It was a fine day—not too warm, but with a gentle, almost undetectable breeze that touched the skin with the

17

lightness of a feather. Such a wind would leave the sand where it lay, unlike those hot winds, laced with dust and grit, that made the eyes water and smart. It was a good day for walking, thought Mma Ramotswe, and today would be the first day she would walk to the office and back again in the late afternoon.

Mma Ramotswe was scrupulously honest, but this did not mean that she was above self-delusion. Had she examined her motives, then she might have been moved to confess that the real reason for walking to work was not so much a determination not to become lazy, but rather a realisation that for the time being it would be best not to use the tiny white van. If she did so, then Mr J. L. B. Matekoni would be sure to hear the noise and would insist on examining the van to see what could be done. And if he did that, then she was certain that the loyal vehicle would be condemned.

That she did not want, and so the decision to walk to work was duly announced to Mr J. L. B. Matekoni.

'That is very good,' he said. 'If people walked to work then they would save a lot of petrol. There would also be fewer cars on the road and not so many traffic jams.'

'And less work for mechanics?' added Mma Ramotswe.

Mr J. L. B. Matekoni shook his head. 'There is always enough work for mechanics,' he said. 'Even if everybody walked, there would still be machines to go wrong.' He thought for a moment. 'And there will always be work for mechanics fixing the bad work that other mechanics have done.'

They looked at one another. There was no doubt about his meaning; he was forever repairing the mistakes of his apprentices, as he had recently told Mma Ramotswe. She said nothing. She was hoping that he would not say anything about the tiny white van; she would confront that problem later. There would be some solution—perhaps a discreet visit to another garage, where the van might be fixed without Mr J. L. B. Matekoni's ever knowing about it. It was even possible that the noise might disappear of its own accord; some engine noises were intermittent, the result of an occlusion of a fuel pipe, perhaps, a tiny piece of grit in the wrong place—there were many innocent explanations. With any luck, this would be the case with the current noise; one never knew with vehicles, as with life in general.

She left home in good time. The journey from Zebra Drive to the offices of the No. 1 Ladies' Detective Agency, shared with Tlokweng Road Speedy Motors, took about ten minutes or less by car but on foot it would take at least forty minutes. Mma Ramotswe decided to allow an hour, although it would not matter too much if she took longer; her first appointment, with Mr Molofololo, was not until eleven o'clock, and there would not be much to do before then. Mma Makutsi would have collected the mail, such as it was, and done whatever filing was left over from yesterday. There were also one or two minor cases that her assistant was working on and she might busy herself with writing reports on these. Mma Makutsi was an enthusiastic writer of reports and maintained a bulging file labelled *Incidental and Interim Reports* that served little purpose in Mma Ramotswe's view, but that kept her busy at slack times. Mma Ramotswe thought of this file as Mma Makutsi's diary, but never described it as such. Her assistant, she remembered, was temperamental, and Mma Ramotswe had not forgotten that she had handed in her resignation not all that long ago. Even if she had stayed out of the office for less than a day, and had returned as if nothing had happened, Mma Ramotswe reminded herself that Mma Makutsi had no real need to work now that she was engaged to be married to Mr Phuti Radiphuti, proprietor of the Double Comfort Furniture Shop and, as such, a man of considerable means. So she was careful not to offend her sometimes prickly assistant, and calling the Incidental and Interim Reports file a diary would undoubtedly have been very offensive.

The walk down Zebra Drive itself was uneventful. Her neighbour's dogs, those strange yellow dogs that Mma Ramotswe did not particularly like, barked at her as if she was any other passer-by, running along the fence at the side of the neighbour's property, baring their teeth in impotent anger. She saw a curtain move in the neighbour's window and heard a shout as the dogs were called in; she waved, and the neighbour returned her greeting, a quick movement of a hand in a still-darkened room.

At the top of Zebra Drive there was more traffic and she had to wait a few moments before she crossed to the other side of the road. The day still had the early-morning feel about it and the air was still sharp with a whiff of wood smoke. There were small huddles of people waiting beside the road for the early minibuses to sway past and a few others walking; domestic employees, Mma Ramotswe thought—cooks, maids, nannies of children— making their way to the well-set houses in the roads near Maru-a-Pula School. One of the women she recognised, a traditionally built woman like herself, who came from somewhere near Kgale Junction and who had served Mma Ramotswe tea when she had called on the Principal of Maru-a-Pula to discuss with him the possibility of her taking part in a careers fair at the school.

'Some of the younger students have put down private detective on their careers form,' the Principal explained. 'So I thought that we should give them an idea of what such work entailed. And you, Mma Ramotswe, are the only private detective in Botswana, are you not?'

'I am always happy to help the school, Mr Taylor,' she said. 'But I am not sure if this is a good idea. If I tell them that it is a good thing to be, then they will want to do this job that I am doing. But where will the work come from?'

The Principal listened carefully. 'But Botswana is growing, Mma Ramotswe. There are many things happening in this country. Surely there will be work for more private detectives.'

Mma Ramotswe thought about this as the traditionally built woman from the school kitchens poured their tea. She looked at the woman, who smiled back at her; there was much that could be said without speaking, especially amongst women. A glance, a movement of the head, a slight shift in pose—all of these could convey a message as eloquently, as volubly, as words might do. The woman wanted to say something, thought Mma Ramotswe, but could not do so in this formal

21

setting. She looked at the woman, but the moment had passed and the Principal had asked a question that needed to be answered.

'Do you not agree with me, Mma Ramotswe?' asked the Principal, passing Mma Ramotswe her tea cup. 'If there is lots of business going on, then there will surely be temptations. Surely there is a need for people to look into that sort of thing.'

'That is true, Rra,' Mma Ramotswe said. 'And I am sometimes asked to check up on dishonest employees. But not all that often.' She paused. 'I am mostly concerned with little things. With the small problems of people's lives.'

'Well, you could talk about that, couldn't you?'

She nodded; she could not say no. Life in Botswana was a matter of asking and doing. People asked one another to do things and they had to agree. Later they could ask back, and the favour would be repaid. Mma Potokwani understood that rule and never hesitated to ask for favours for the children at the orphan farm, as Mr J. L. B. Matekoni knew only too well, being regularly called out to fix various pieces of machinery, including the van used to transport the children on outings. And there had been reciprocation in that case, if one counted generous slices of fruit cake as reciprocation; Mma Ramotswe would have called the cake a bribe, given Mr J. L. B. Matekoni's well-known weakness for such treats, but reciprocation was perhaps a politer word.

Now, just short of the corner that marked the edge of the Sun Hotel gardens, Mma Ramotswe came face to face with the woman who had served her tea in Mr Taylor's office. She hesitated, as did the other woman, who had recognised her too. The traditional greetings were exchanged and then there was a moment of awkward silence. On a flamboyant tree behind a fence, a small, glossy bird watched them, the sun on its purple-black plumage.

The silence was broken by Mma Ramotswe. 'I am Precious Ramotswe. I saw you, Mma, in the office at the school. Do you remember?'

The woman seemed pleased to have been remembered. Such people can be invisible to others. 'I remember that well, Mma. You were talking to Mr Taylor. He is a kind man.'

'Yes,' said Mma Ramotswe. 'I have heard that.' She paused, searching the woman's expression. Yes, it was there. It was unmistakable. 'Do you want to talk to me, Mma?'

The woman gave a start. She was nervous. 'To talk, Mma?'

Mma Ramotswe reached out a hand. She did not touch the other woman, but held her hand in such a position that she could take it if she wished. 'I think that you are troubled, my sister,' she said. 'It is my job to listen to the troubles of others. Did you know that?'

The woman looked down at the ground. She did not take the proffered hand and Mma Ramotswe let it drop back to her side.

'I know that, Mma. But I am not a rich lady. I do not have money.'

'That does not matter,' said Mma Ramotswe. 'I am your sister, Mma.'

It was her way of expressing the old bonds that had always held the country together; a subtle, usually unspoken sense of mutual interest and respect, that people could forget about, but that was still there and could be invoked by those who held with the old ways. *I am your sister*. There was no simpler or more effective way of expressing a whole philosophy of life.

The woman looked up. 'It is very good of you, Mma, but I cannot talk now. I have my work to do. I have to get to the school.'

Mma Ramotswe nodded. 'Well, as long as you know that I shall listen to you. Do you know where my place is?'

The woman turned and pointed over her shoulder. 'It is over on that side. On the Tlokweng Road. Next to a big garage.'

Mma Ramotswe smiled. Tlokweng Road Speedy Motors could hardly be called a big garage, but she knew what the woman meant. When one was down at the bottom of the heap, then any business, even a small one like the garage, could seem big and important.

'Yes,' she said. 'It is beside a garage. But it is not a big office, and if you ever come to see me you will be made a cup of redbush tea. You are always making tea for other people; you will have to let us make tea for you for a change.'

The woman smiled at this, and then continued on her way. Mma Ramotswe looked at her watch. There was still plenty of time but she suspected that walking to work would not be quite as quick as she had imagined.

*   *   *

By the time she came within sight of Tlokweng Road Speedy Motors and the No. 1 Ladies' Detective Agency, Mma Ramotswe had developed

24

a raging thirst. Her feet, she noted with satisfaction, felt perfectly comfortable—she had her flat shoes to thank for that—and she still had plenty of energy. It was just thirst that troubled her, and that would be easily dealt with when Mma Makutsi put on the kettle for the first cup of tea of the working day.

As she approached the garage, Charlie emerged from the inspection pit, wiping oil off his hands.

'So, Mma Ramotswe,' he called out as she approached. 'Has your old van broken down at last? Do you want me to take the boss's truck to fetch it?'

Mma Ramotswe frowned. 'There is nothing wrong. I have simply decided to walk to work. It is better to walk, you know.'

Charlie looked at her incredulously. 'It is better to walk, you say, Mma?'

'Yes, Charlie, that is what I said. And you two could do to walk a bit more.'

'I am always walking, Mma,' said the younger apprentice, who had appeared behind Charlie. 'I walk over two kilometres to the bus stop every day.'

'That is very good, Fanwell,' said Mma Ramotswe. 'You are not lazy.'

'Nor am I,' interjected Charlie. 'I may not walk very much, but why walk if God has given us cars and buses? What's the point?'

Mma Ramotswe took a handkerchief out of her pocket and mopped her brow. 'Exercise,' she said. 'That's the point.'

Charlie sniggered. 'I get a lot of exercise, Mma. I get plenty of exercise by dancing with girls. One, two, three! Like that. That is very good exercise.'

The younger apprentice looked at Charlie with surprise. 'Is that true, Charlie?'

'Of course it's not true. Nothing he says is true.' It was the voice of Mma Makutsi, who had appeared in the office doorway, holding out a mug of tea to Mma Ramotswe.

Mma Ramotswe took the mug gratefully. 'I am very thirsty, Mma,' she said. 'It is kind of you to have this ready for me.'

'If you drove,' said Charlie, 'then you wouldn't feel so thirsty. It is too hot to walk.'

'But not too hot to dance?' snapped Mma Makutsi.

Charlie did not reply, but Mma Ramotswe heard him whisper to Fanwell: 'Who would dance with her? Nobody. Only that Phuti Radiphuti, and his feet are like elephants' feet. Big dancer. Hot steps.'

Fortunately, Mma Makutsi had gone back into the office and did not hear this remark. Mma Ramotswe gave Charlie a reproachful look. 'You should not say things like that, Charlie. It is not kind.'

'She says things about me,' the apprentice replied.

Mma Ramotswe sighed. 'You will learn one day, maybe soon, that what others do is never an excuse. Have you not heard of turning the other cheek?'

Charlie was unrepentant. 'I have not heard of that.'

Mma Ramotswe began to explain, but could tell that what she said was falling on deaf ears.

'I would never do that,' said Charlie. 'It would be very foolish, Mma Ramotswe. You show your other cheek and, whack, they hit you on that

26

one too.'

CHAPTER THREE

THE BEAUTIFUL GAME

'He is here now,' said Mma Makutsi, peering out of the window. 'That is his car.'

Mma Ramotswe made a conscious effort not to look up from her desk. 'I take it that it is a Mercedes-Benz, Mma,' she muttered.

Mma Makutsi laughed. 'It is a very big one, Mma. It is one of the biggest Mercedes-Benzes that I have ever seen.'

'He is a big man, I hear,' said Mma Ramotswe. 'You would never find a man like that driving around in a van like mine.'

Mma Makutsi agreed. She shared Mma Ramotswe's views on cars—that they should be small, faithful, and designed to get one as simply and cheaply as possible from one place to another. When she had a car herself—and Phuti had spoken about getting her one—then she would certainly not ask for a Mercedes-Benz, but would go for one of those small cars that look as if they could as easily go backwards as forwards, so indistinguishable were their fronts and their backs. And she would prefer it to be a modest colour: she had seen a very nice lilac-coloured car the other day that would suit her very well. She had wondered about that. Somebody at the factory had clearly said: Now let us paint this car a suitable colour for a lady. No man would choose lilac, she

27

imagined, and it would be left to a lady to give such a car a home; which she would, and readily so.

'Why is it that men are so keen on large cars, Mma?' she asked, as she watched the driver of the car step out and open the rear passenger door. 'Could it be that they feel they need such cars because they do not think they are big and strong enough?'

'Maybe,' said Mma Ramotswe. 'Men and boys are all the same, I think, Mma Makutsi. They need to play. As do ladies, of course. Ladies play in their own way.'

'Maybe we are all the same,' mused Mma Makutsi. 'But when you look at Charlie . . .'

Her observations were cut short by the sound of footsteps and a knocking outside. Mma Ramotswe now glanced up and nodded in the direction of the door. 'Please let him in, Mma Makutsi,' she said. 'I am ready for Mr Leungo Molofololo.'

Mma Makutsi stood up, straightened her skirt, and crossed the room.

'One moment please, Rra,' she said to the man at the door. 'I shall find out if Mma Ramotswe is ready to see you.'

She glanced over her shoulder, as if to seek confirmation. Mma Ramotswe nodded. She had often explained to Mma Makutsi that such pretence was unnecessary, but her assistant insisted on carrying out the charade when important visitors came and she had given up trying to stop her. For her part, Mma Ramotswe did not stand on ceremony; nor did she try to give anybody the impression that the business was larger and grander than it really was. 'People will judge us by our results,' she said to Mma Makutsi.

'Results are the important thing.'

Mma Makutsi contemplated this. 'That is a pity, Mma,' she observed. 'Because our results are sometimes not very good.'

Mma Ramotswe shook her head. 'But I think they are, Mma. Sometimes we do not find out exactly what the client wants, but we find out what they need to know. There is a difference, you know.' She thought of the case of Mma Sebina, who had been adopted and had come to them with the request that they find her real family. They had succeeded in tracing a brother who turned out not to be a brother after all. At one level that appeared to be a failure, but then when Mma Sebina and the man she had thought was her brother decided that they were really rather fond of one another—fond enough to get married—then that had surely been a happy result. And then there had been the case of Happy Bapetsi, one of their very first cases, in which they had discovered that Happy's father was an impostor. Or Kremlin, the frequenter of the Go-Go Handsome Man's Bar, the philandering husband; Mma Ramotswe had proved him to be exactly that—a philanderer—and even if that was not the outcome that Kremlin's wife wanted, it was surely better for her to know. So success and failure in the private detection business were not always as clear-cut as they might seem, but again it had been difficult to persuade Mma Makutsi of this and the subject had been dropped.

Now, moving aside to let Mr Leungo Molofololo enter the office, Mma Makutsi said, 'Mma Ramotswe, this is your ten o'clock appointment.'

Mr Leungo Molofololo looked at his watch. 'And I am here at precisely four minutes past ten, you will observe, Mma. I like to be punctual, you see.'

'That is a great virtue, Rra,' said Mma Ramotswe, rising from her seat and gesturing for him to sit down.

'Yes,' said Mr Leungo Molofololo. 'If only more people cultivated that virtue in Africa, then life would work more smoothly. You have heard of the Germans, Mma? I have been told that everything they do runs on time. Bang, bang. Like that. On the minute.'

'That is the Swiss, Rra,' said Mma Makutsi from behind.

Mr Leungo Molofololo turned and looked at Mma Makutsi, who smiled back at him. 'They may be very punctual, Mma. It is possible that both the Swiss and the Germans are very punctual—and there may be others. We do not necessarily know. I was, however, talking about the Germans but thank you, Mma, for your help there.'

'The Swiss are always making clocks,' Mma Makutsi went on. 'That is perhaps why they are so punctual. If there are many clocks, then . . .'

'Thank you, Mma Makutsi,' said Mma Ramotswe firmly. 'Perhaps you will be kind enough to make tea for all of us so that Mr Molofololo will be able to drink tea while he speaks to me.' She emphasised the *me*, hoping that Mma Makutsi would take the proper inference; but she had her doubts.

Mr Leungo Molofololo turned back to address Mma Ramotswe. 'I don't know if you know anything about me,' he said. 'You may have seen my name in the papers.' He paused. 'Have you?'

'Not only have I seen your name there,' said

30

Mma Ramotswe, 'but I have also seen your photograph, Rra. Last week I saw you handing over a big cheque to the nurses' charity. That was very kind of you.'

'They are good people,' said Mr Molofololo. 'And I admire the nursing profession. If I had been born a woman, Mma—which I am happy to say I was not—then I would have been a nurse, I think.'

Mma Ramotswe glanced at Mma Makutsi, whose eyes flashed at this. She inclined her head slightly, a sign that she hoped would be understood by Mma Makutsi, a sign that said, *I shall handle this.*

'You might have been quite happy to be born a woman, Rra,' she said politely.

Mr Molofololo's answer came quickly. 'No, I would not. I would have been very sad.'

Mma Ramotswe laughed. 'I think that most people are happy with what they are. Men are happy to be born men, and women are happy to be born women. It is not better to be the one or the other, although I must say that I am very relieved indeed that I was not born a man.'

Mr Molofololo opened his mouth to say something but Mma Ramotswe continued quickly, 'And as for being a nurse, well, Rra, there are many other things that a woman can be these days. Everything, in fact. Would you not like to have been a doctor if you had been born a woman? Or a pilot with Air Botswana—how about that?'

Mr Molofololo was silent for a moment. Then, 'You're quite right, Mma. My daughter is always saying to me, *Daddy, you must remember that the world is not just there for you. It is there for minorities too.* No, you are right, Mma, we must remember the rights of women.'

'Who are not in a minority,' said Mma Makutsi from behind her desk. 'In fact, there are more women than there are men because men die earlier than women. They die earlier because they drink too much and sit about. So we are the majority, Rra.'

Mr Molofololo cast his eyes up towards the ceiling. 'Not in the world of football, Mma,' he said. 'And that is what I have come to see *Mma Ramotswe* about.'

Mma Ramotswe smiled at him apologetically. 'Mma Makutsi is an assistant detective, Rra. She is very good at investigating a wide range of matters. And she is the fiancée of Phuti Radiphuti. You will probably know the father of that man . . .'

Her remarks had the desired effect. Mr Molofololo half turned in his seat and gave Mma Makutsi a nod. 'I'm very happy to meet you, Mma. I did not know that it was you. Mr Radiphuti—the older one—is a friend of many years.'

'That is very good,' said Mma Ramotswe. And it was; Mma Ramotswe liked people to know one another, and if the bond between them went back over more than one generation, then all the better. That was how it had always been in Botswana, where the links between people, those profound connections of blood and lineage, spread criss-cross over the human landscape, binding one to another in reliance, trust and sheer familiarity. At one time there had been no strangers in Botswana; everybody fitted in somehow, even if tenuously and on the margins. Now there were strangers, and the bonds had been weakened by drift to the towns and by other things too: by the conduct that had sired the wave of children who had no idea who their father, or their father's people, might be; by the cruel ravages of the disease that made orphans in a country where the very concept of an orphan had been barely known, as there had always been aunts and grandmothers aplenty to fill the breach. Yes, all that had changed, but in spite of it, the old bonds survived, as she saw now in Mr Molofololo's recognition of the fact that Mma Makutsi was not just a secretary given to irritating interjections, but a person with a place.

'Football,' said Mr Molofololo. 'Or you can call it soccer, if you like. The beautiful game. You know that it is called that, Mma? That is what they call football.'

Mma Ramotswe did not know that. She had never been to a football match, although she had seen boys, including Puso, playing it and had watched for a few minutes here and there. Was it beautiful? She supposed that it was—in a manner of speaking. They were always very skilful, those soccer players, as the nicknames they often bore revealed. She had seen these mentioned recently in the newspaper, when a football player called Fast-Dancer Galeboe had been pictured at a function talking to another player called High-Jump Boseja. Those nicknames at least gave some indication of the talents of the player in question; others seemed less obvious. She had read about Joel 'Twelve Volts' Koko of the Township Rollers, or Sekhana 'Fried Chicken' Molwantwa of the Extension Gunners. She could not imagine why Mr Koko should be called Twelve Volts, although she could presume that Mr Molwantwa had a taste for fried chicken. Perhaps the whole thing was to do with

33

the way men got on with one another; they often laughed and slapped each other on the back or pretended to kick one another. Perhaps it was to do with all that.

'I am afraid that I do not know much about football, Rra,' Mma Ramotswe said. 'But I can understand why it should be called the beautiful game—with all that running around and dodging in and out. That might be called beautiful, I suppose.'

'I have never understood the attraction myself,' chipped in Mma Makutsi. 'Why make such a fuss about kicking a ball up and down a field?'

Mr Molofololo appeared to take this in good humour. 'It is because you ladies are women,' he said. 'It is not something that women understand.' He paused, and then added hurriedly, 'Of course there are many things that men do not understand. They do not understand some of the things that women understand. Such as . . .' He trailed off.

'Yes, Rra?' prompted Mma Ramotswe.

Mr Molofololo waved a hand in the air. 'There are many things. Women's business. Shoes maybe. That sort of thing.'

Mma Ramotswe and Mma Makutsi exchanged glances. He is right, thought Mma Ramotswe; men do not understand shoes—not completely, not in the deep way in which women understand them. For men, shoes were simply things you put on your feet; for women, shoes were . . . well, there was no time to go into that.

Mr Molofololo moved on. 'Perhaps it would be best, Mma, if I told you a little bit about myself. Then you will understand why this problem that I have come to see you about is such a big one.' He paused, and put a hand over his heart. Mma Ramotswe noticed the starched cuff of his shirt and the heavy gold cuff-links. It was a strange thing about rich men, she reflected. If they have made the money themselves, then they are usually keen to let you know just how much money they have; if they had got it from their father, or even their grandfather, then they often never mentioned it. Mr Molofololo had obviously made his money himself.

'This problem,' he went on, 'hurts me here. Right here—in my heart.'

Mma Ramotswe inclined her head gravely. Everybody who consulted her was, in their way, hurting—even this rich man with his big Mercedes-Benz and his expensive cuff-links. Human hurt was like lightning; it did not choose its targets, but struck, with rough equality and little regard to position, achievement, or moral desert.

'I have worked very hard, Mma Ramotswe,' Mr Molofololo went on. 'Ever since I was a small boy, I have worked. I herded cattle, you know, the same as all small boys from the villages. We were poor people, you understand. And then I went to school and I worked harder than any of the other boys. When the other boys were playing football I studied and studied. Then when the school Principal asked me what I wanted to be, I said that I would be an accountant. I had read somewhere about CAs, and I said, *I will be a CA one day*. And that is what I now am. I am a chartered accountant, but I am also a businessman. I have many shops. Here. There. Many shops.'

Mma Ramotswe noticed that Mma Makutsi was listening intently to this, and she knew why. Her

35

assistant had worked her way out of poverty, and had achieved ninety-seven per cent in the final examinations of the Botswana Secretarial College by dint of sheer, unremitting hard work. If Mma Makutsi identified with Mr Molofololo's story, it was because it was her story too, except for the herding, and the football, the chartered accountancy, and the shops—except for all the details, in fact.

'But you know how it is, Mma,' Mr Molofololo continued. 'When you are a success in business you begin to think of the things that you've missed while you were working so hard. That is why you hear people say: *I have been working, working, working, and now my children are grown up and I did not see that happen*. Have you heard people say that, Mma?'

Mma Ramotswe had not, but she could imagine that people might indeed say it, so she nodded.

Mr Molofololo leaned back in his chair. 'And do you know what I thought, Mma Ramotswe? I will tell you. I thought: I never played football, and now it is too late. That is what I thought. You can't have a man in his fifties running round the football field, can you? His heart will say no. So it was too late.'

He paused, and then, with the air of one making an important announcement, he said, 'But if it was too late to play football myself, it was not too late to buy a football team, Mma. Hah! So I bought a team that had not been doing very well—a nothing, useless team—and I got rid of all those lazy players and put in new ones who wanted to score lots of goals. And that's how the Kalahari Swoopers were born. Now you see us right up there, up at the top

36

of the league most of the time, or number two at least. Until recently, that is. I did that. I did all that myself.'

Mma Makutsi had been silent. But now she asked, 'You did that yourself, Rra? You played after all?'

Mr Molofololo ignored the question at first, but then gave an answer. 'No, not me, Mma. I am the owner. The football is played by the football players. And we have a coach, a very good one. He tells the men what tactics will work best.'

'You must be very proud of your team, Rra,' said Mma Ramotswe. 'Even I have heard of it. And I am just a woman.'

Mr Molofololo did not notice the irony. 'Well, there you are,' he said. 'That goes to show, doesn't it?'

Mma Ramotswe knew that if she did not say something, Mma Makutsi would say, 'Goes to show what?' So she asked him how his team was doing. Why were they no longer at the top of the league?

It was the right question to ask, as it was this, he explained, that had brought him to see her. 'Something has gone badly wrong,' he said. 'A few months ago we started to lose a lot of games. At first I thought that it was just a little spell of bad luck; one cannot win every time, I suppose. But then it continued, and we are now going further and further down the league table. People are laughing at us. They say, *Look at the Swoopers. They cannot swoop. No more swooping there*. It is very painful, Mma, and I feel very ashamed of my team.'

'That is very sad,' said Mma Ramotswe. 'To

build something up and then see it be destroyed is not a very nice experience, I think.'

He was grateful for the sympathy. 'Thank you, Mma. I'm sure that you can imagine what it would be like to see your own business suddenly go downhill. Imagine it. You solve all those cases and then suddenly there are no more solutions. It would not feel good, would it?'

Mma Ramotswe was tactful. 'There are always reversals in business. It is not the fault of the person running the business—or, at least, it's not always their fault.'

This comment seemed to engage Mr Molofololo, who suddenly became animated. 'It is definitely not their fault, Mma! And in this case it is not the fault of my players—or most of them. I have the same young men playing for me, and they are as good as ever. But whatever they do, something seems to go badly wrong. Penalties are given away unnecessarily or the defence doesn't quite work out. There are many reasons.'

Mma Ramotswe held up a hand. 'If it's a game, Rra, then surely anything can happen. Maybe things will improve.'

Mr Molofololo shook his head disconsolately. 'I would like to think that,' he said. 'But I'm afraid that we're doomed. I do not think that things will get any better until . . .'

Mma Ramotswe looked at him expectantly. 'Until what, Rra?'

'Until we find out who the traitor is.'

Mma Ramotswe waited for him to expand on this, but he simply looked at her angrily, as if blaming her in some way for his team's misfortunes. Was he one of those people, she

38

wondered, who see enemies at every turn? She had known somebody like that once; he had suspected everybody of plotting against him. Perhaps Mr Molofololo saw traitors everywhere, all of them intent on letting him down.

'Perhaps you should tell me about this traitor,' she said gently. 'Is it a business rival of yours, maybe?'

This suggestion seemed to make Mr Molofololo even crosser. 'I don't know, Mma,' he said, somewhat peevishly. 'It may be somebody like that behind the traitor. Who knows? The real problem is that there is a traitor in the team.'

'Somebody who wants you to lose?' Mma Ramotswe had heard of people who fixed games—there had been some row about this happening in cricket in South Africa and it had got into the local papers. But would the same thing happen in football in Gaborone? She wondered whether the stakes would be high enough; perhaps they were. Perhaps it was a matter of Mercedes-Benzes; they seemed to come into these things a great deal.

Mr Molofololo folded his hands in his lap. 'Yes, Mma Ramotswe, I'm afraid that may be true. In fact, I'm sure that it's true. There is somebody in the team who wants us to lose and is making very sure that we do.'

Mr Molofololo stopped speaking, and there was silence. Outside, in the acacia tree behind the office, a dove cooed—the small Cape dove that had taken up residence in the tree and cooed for a mate who never came.

Mma Ramotswe spread her hands. 'I don't know, Rra, if I am the best person to find out what is going on here,' she said.

'But you're a detective,' protested Mr Molofololo. 'And I have asked around, Mma. Everybody has said to me: you go to that Mma Ramotswe—she is the one who can find things out. That is what they said.'

It was flattering to Mma Ramotswe to hear that her reputation had spread, but she knew nothing at all about football and it seemed to her that it would be impossible to detect something as subtle and devious as match-fixing. It would be difficult enough for her to work out which direction the team was playing in, let alone to discover who was deliberately not doing his best.

'I may be a detective, Rra,' she explained, 'but this is a very special thing you are asking me to do. How can I find out who this . . . this traitor is if I know nothing about football? I cannot sit there and say, *See that? See what is going on over there—that is very suspicious*. I cannot do that.'

'And I cannot either,' said Mma Makutsi. 'I know nothing about football either.'

Mr Molofololo sighed. 'I'm not asking you to do that, Mma,' he said. 'I'm asking you to look into the private lives of the players. Find out who is being paid money to do this—because money will be changing hands, I'm sure of it.'

This changed everything. 'I can certainly do that, Rra,' said Mma Ramotswe. 'Indeed, that is what we do rather well, isn't it, Mma Makutsi?'

Mma Makutsi nodded emphatically. 'We often find out where men are hiding their money when it comes to divorce,' she said. 'Men are very cunning, Rra. But we find out where the money is.'

Mr Molofololo raised an eyebrow. 'I'm sure you do,' he said.

40

'So we shall be happy to act for you,' said Mma Ramotswe. 'We will need details of all the players. We shall need to know exactly where they live and I need to be able to have some contact with the team. Can you think of any suitable cover for me?'

Mr Molofololo thought for a moment. 'We have a lady who gives massages to the players,' he said. 'She helps them if they pull a muscle or something like that. But she also helps to keep their limbs in good working order. You could be her assistant, perhaps. She has worked for me for many years and is very discreet.'

'That is important,' said Mma Makutsi from behind her desk. 'One does not want a lady who talks too much.'

*   *   *

At the end of that day, at five o'clock, when the whole of Gaborone streamed out of its shops and offices and other places of work, when the sun began to sink low over the Kalahari to the west, Mma Ramotswe locked the office behind her and walked, with Mma Makutsi, on to the Tlokweng Road. Mma Makutsi would catch a minibus there, one of those swaying, overloaded vehicles that plied their trade along the roads that led into the city, and she said to Mma Ramotswe, 'Why walk all the way, Mma? Come with me on the minibus and then you can get off when we get to the crossroads and walk from there.'

She was tempted. It had been a busy day, what with Mr Molofololo and several other clients who had slipped in without an appointment, and all she wanted now was to get home. But she had said that

41

she would walk, and walk she would.

'No thank you, Mma. It is good exercise, you see. It's important that people in Botswana should get exercise. We talked about that already.'

Mma Makutsi smiled. 'But it's also important,' she said, 'that people in Botswana get back home in good time. It's important that they have time to cook themselves a good dinner. It's important that they do not get covered in dust from too much walking. All of these things are important.'

Mma Ramotswe just smiled. 'I hope that you sleep well tonight, Mma. I shall see you tomorrow morning.'

And with that they bade their farewells and Mma Makutsi watched Mma Ramotswe begin to walk along the road back towards town. She admired her employer, who was far stronger, she thought, than she was herself. I would never walk if I had the chance of getting into a car or a minibus. No, I would not, and that is because Mma Ramotswe is a strong and determined lady and I am just one of these ladies who blow with the wind. She paused; she was not sure that this was the right metaphor. For a moment she imagined Mma Ramotswe being buffeted by a strong wind, one of the hot, dry winds that come from far off in the bush, far over on the other side of the border, from hills that she could not name and had never seen. She saw the wind ruffle Mma Ramotswe's skirt and blouse, inflating them briefly; but Mma Ramotswe stood firm, while all about her acacia trees were bending and leaves whirling in mad vortices. Mma Ramotswe stood firm, even when lesser people, thin, insubstantial people, were being toppled and bowled over by the wind. That was Mma Ramotswe, her rock.

Unaware of Mma Makutsi's fantasy, Mma Ramotswe made her way slowly along the edge of the road. The traffic was light in that direction, as most of the cars were coming out of town, heading back to the sprawling village of Tlokweng. She was now passing the eucalyptus trees that stretched out towards the dam to the south; she drove past these trees every day and she thought that she knew them well. But now, on foot, it was as if she saw them for the first time. She loved their scent, that slightly prickly scent that reminded her of the handkerchiefs that her father's cousin used. She would put a few drops of eucalyptus oil on to the cloth and let the young Precious smell them. 'That keeps away colds,' the cousin said. 'If you put eucalyptus oil on your handkerchief your nose is safe. Always.'

Mma Ramotswe smiled at the memory. She did not think that eucalyptus oil made a difference; she had read somewhere that nothing made a difference to colds other than washing your hands after you had touched a person suffering from one. People believed all manner of things, in the face of all the evidence, but if they did not, well, what then? What if we stopped believing in things that we could not prove? We had to believe in something, she thought. We had to believe in kindness and courtesy and telling the truth; we had to believe in the old Botswana values—all of these things could not be proved in the way in which one could prove that nothing made a difference to colds, and yet we had to believe them.

Such thoughts to be thinking while walking along the side of the Tlokweng Road; but at least they distracted her, even if only temporarily, from

43

a growing feeling of discomfort in her right foot. Now, as Mma Ramotswe turned off into the area known as the village, to walk along Odi Drive, she realised that what she was developing was a blister, and a painful one at that. She stopped, crouched down and took off her shoe, feeling gingerly for that place where she thought the pain came from. Yes, the skin was raised there; it was a blister.

She wondered whether she should remove her right shoe, or possibly both shoes. There was a time when she would have thought nothing of that; as a child and then as a young woman she would happily walk about unshod, particularly in the sand, which gave such a fine feeling to the soles of the feet. But now her feet had become softer and the very earth seemed to have become thornier and less hospitable.

She replaced her shoe and began to walk down Odi Drive. The blister was quite painful now and she was having to put less weight on that leg, resulting in a hobbling motion. Zebra Drive was still a long way away—at least twenty minutes, she thought, and she could imagine what her foot would be like at the end of that.

She was now only a few yards—even if painful yards—from the Moffat house on the corner. She would go and see the Moffats, she decided; if the doctor was in, then he might even take a look at the blister and give her some cream for it. And if she asked, she was sure Mma Moffat would drive her home and save her continuing agony.

Dr Moffat was at home, and while Mma Moffat made tea for Mma Ramotswe, he examined her foot.

'A very bad blister,' he said. 'But I think we can

save the foot.'

Mma Ramotswe looked up in alarm and saw that Dr Moffat was smiling. 'You worried me, Rra.'

'Just a little joke, Mma Ramotswe,' he said, peeling the covering off a small square of sticking plaster. 'Your foot's fine. But tell me: why are you walking? What's wrong with your tiny white van?'

Mma Ramotswe hesitated. 'Oh, Dr Moffat, I am very sad. I am very, very sad. My van . . .'

'Have you had an accident?'

'No, not an accident. My van is an old one. It has been my friend for many years—right from the time I came to Gaborone. And now it is like an old cow standing under a tree waiting for the end to come. I don't know . . .'

She faltered. She did not know what to do, and now she wept for the van that she loved so much. It was ridiculous, she thought, a grown woman weeping for a van. But Dr Moffat did not think it ridiculous; he had seen so much of human suffering in all its shapes and sizes and he knew how easy it was for people to cry. So he and Mma Moffat, who had come in with a cup of tea for their visitor, comforted her and talked to her about the little white van.

'One thing's very certain,' said Dr Moffat. 'It's the same for humans as it is for vans. When something needs to be fixed, don't just deny it. Go and see somebody—a doctor for a person, a mechanic for a van.'

'Mr J. L. B. Matekoni will just tell me it has to go. I know he will.'

'Then speak to one of those young men—his apprentices. Get him to fix it for you.'

Mma Ramotswe was silent as she contemplated

45

this suggestion. She would never lie to Mr J. L. B. Matekoni, but that did not mean that she had to tell him *everything*.

CHAPTER FOUR

MMA MAKUTSI MAKES PERI-PERI CHICKEN

That evening, while Mma Ramotswe nursed the painful blister on her right heel, Mma Makutsi was busy in her kitchen, cooking dinner for her fiancé, Mr Phuti Radiphuti, proprietor of the Double Comfort Furniture Shop and owner, too, of a large herd of fine cattle built up by his father, the older Mr Radiphuti. Mma Makutsi knew what Phuti Radiphuti's culinary tastes were and had recently discovered that he was particularly partial to peri-peri chicken, a dish that the Portuguese had dreamed up in Mozambique and Angola. From there it had spread into other countries, including Botswana, where it was a favourite amongst those who liked their food to be scathingly hot. Phuti was one of these, she thought, and could happily chew on the most stinging of chilli peppers without the need of a glass of water.

'You'll get used to it, Grace,' he said. 'You will not feel it at all. Peri-peri chicken, vindaloo curries—everything. It will all taste equally good.'

She was doubtful, but for Phuti's sake was still prepared to put up with what she thought to be excessively fiery dishes; and now she was making one of these, dropping several large pinches of

46

flaked chilli into the marinade of oil and lemon juice that she had prepared shortly before Phuti's arrival.

She dipped a finger into the sauce and then dabbed it against her tongue. Immediately she felt an intense stinging sensation and reached for a glass of water to cool the burning. How can he do it? she asked herself. This made her reflect on how often one had to pose that question about men. They did all sorts of inexplicable things and women were always asking themselves the same question: how can they do it?

When Phuti arrived half an hour later, the chicken was almost ready. Phuti sat at her table, which was covered with a new yellow tablecloth she had recently bought, and watched Mma Makutsi attend to the final preparations.

'I am a very lucky man to be marrying somebody who can make peri-peri chicken,' he announced. 'I always wanted to meet such a lady.'

She laughed. 'Would you not marry me if I could not make peri-peri chicken?'

Phuti thought this very amusing. He was not quite as quick as Mma Makutsi and he enjoyed her ability to make light-hearted comments such as this. He would have liked to have been able to reply with some witty riposte, but what could he say? Of course he would have married her, irrespective of her ability to cook peri-peri chicken. Indeed, he had not even known about that until after he had proposed.

'I would marry you,' he said, 'even if you could cook nothing—nothing at all! I would marry you even if you wore glasses, which you do, of course.'

For a while nothing was said as both of them

tried to work out the significance of the last remark. Then Phuti cleared his throat. 'Of course I do not mind glasses, and yours are very pretty, Grace. That is what I think.'

Mma Makutsi stirred the peri-peri chicken rather more aggressively than perhaps was necessary. 'The chicken is almost ready, Phuti,' she said. 'I will serve you now.'

They ate in silence and it was several minutes before Phuti spoke. 'When I said . . .' he began. 'I didn't mean . . .'

'Of course not. I didn't think that you meant that.'

During the ensuing silence Mma Makutsi drank several glasses of water. It felt to her as if a hot iron had been run across her tongue, and the water, curiously enough, seemed only to make each successive mouthful seem more fiery. When the chicken was finished, she served a dessert of pineapple and custard that she knew Phuti would like, and this seemed to dispel the gloom that had settled over the table.

'My favourite too!' enthused Phuti.

She ladled a few more spoonfuls of the custard on to his plate. 'Did anything happen in the furniture store today?' she asked.

Phuti wiped a speck of custard away from the corner of his mouth. 'We took delivery of a new consignment of chairs,' he said. 'They came from a factory over in Durban, and when we opened the crate we saw that the legs had fallen off a number of them. Can you believe that, Grace? Four days out of the factory and the legs have fallen off.'

'That is very bad workmanship,' said Mma Makutsi. 'What can those people be thinking about?'

Phuti shook his head sadly. 'It is happening all the time now. People do not care how they make things. A little bit of glue and they think that a chair will hold together with that. It's very dangerous.'

'Particularly for traditionally built people,' said Mma Makutsi. 'What if somebody like Mma Ramotswe sat in one of those chairs? She could fall right down.'

Phuti agreed. 'I would not like to see Mma Ramotswe sitting on one of those chairs,' he said. 'She is safer in the chair that she has, even if it is very old. Sometimes old things are best. An old chair and an old bed. They can be very good.'

Mma Makutsi did not welcome this mention of beds. Her embarrassment over the bed she had ruined by leaving it out in the rain had not entirely disappeared, and she felt the back of her neck become warm even to think about it.

'Chairs,' she said quickly. 'Yes, old chairs can be very comfortable. Although I do not think that the chair I have in the office is very comfortable. It gives me a sore back at the end of the day, I'm afraid. It is not the same shape as I am, you see.'

Phuti frowned. 'You are a very nice shape, Grace. I have always said that. It is the chair that is wrong.'

The compliment was appreciated, and she smiled at her fiancé. 'Thank you, Phuti. Yes, the chair is very old. It has been there since the very beginning, when we had that old office over near Kgale Hill.'

'Then I must give you a new one,' said Phuti firmly. 'I will bring one round to the office tomorrow. We have a whole new section for office furniture in the shop, and there are many fine-looking chairs. I will bring you a good one.'

She thanked him, but then thought: what about Mma Ramotswe? What would she feel if she saw her assistant getting a new chair while she was stuck with her old one? She could always raise this issue with Phuti Radiphuti, but if she did so he might feel that she was being greedy: one did not accept a present with one hand and at the same time hold out the other on behalf of somebody else. *Thank you, Rra, for the nice chair you have given me, and now how about one for my friend, Mma Ramotswe?* That would not do.

While Mma Makutsi wrestled with this question of etiquette, Phuti Radiphuti was clearly warming to the subject of chairs. It was always like that when he talked about furniture, she thought—his eyes lit up. And he did enjoy talking about furniture, in the same way as so many men talked about football. That was a good thing: if one had to choose between marrying a man who talked about furniture and one who talked about football, then there was no doubt in Mma Makutsi's mind as to which she preferred. There was so little one could say about football without repeating oneself, whereas there were a lot of things to be said about furniture, or at least some things.

'What colour?' asked Phuti. 'What colour would you like your chair to be?'

Mma Makutsi was surprised by the question. She had always assumed that office chairs were black, or possibly sometimes grey: her chair at the office was somewhere in between these two colours—it was difficult to tell now, with all the use it had seen.

'Do you have green?' she asked. 'I have always wanted a green chair.'

'There is certainly green,' said Phuti. 'There is a very good chair that comes in green.'

It was now time for second helpings of pineapple and custard. Then, with the dessert cleared away and the tea cups set out at the ready, Mma Makutsi put on the kettle while Phuti sat back in his chair with the air of a man replete.

'And something else happened at the shop today,' he announced. 'Something else that I think you will be interested to hear about.'

Mma Makutsi reached for the tea caddy, an ancient round tin on which the word *Mafeking* had been printed underneath a picture of a street and a line of parked cars. 'You have had a busy day,' she said.

'Yes,' said Phuti. 'And this other thing that happened has something to do with our being busy. We have taken on a new person.'

Mma Makutsi ladled tea into the teapot. One spoon for each mouth, she muttered, and one for the pot. 'So what will he do, this new person?' she asked.

'She,' corrected Phuti. 'She will be assistant manager in charge of beds. We have decided to start selling beds again and we need somebody who can sell beds. It has to be the right sort of person.'

'And what sort of person is that?' asked Mma Makutsi.

Phuti appeared to be momentarily embarrassed. 'A glamorous person,' he said, smiling apologetically. 'Everybody in the furniture business says the same thing: if you want to sell expensive beds, get a very beautiful lady to do it for you.'

Mma Makutsi laughed. 'That is why advertisements for cars always have a picture of a beautiful girl,' she said. 'It is so easy to see what they are trying to do.'

'I think you are right,' said Phuti. 'So we advertised a sales post and we had thirty people applying for it, Mma. Thirty. There must be many people who would like to sell beds.'

'Lazy people, perhaps,' said Mma Makutsi. 'Lazy people will like to sell beds; people who are not lazy will like to sell running shoes.'

Phuti absorbed this insight. It was probably correct, he thought.

'But one of them was very good,' he continued. 'She is a graduate of the Botswana Secretarial College. Eighty per cent in the final examinations.'

Mma Makutsi hesitated, her hand poised above the kettle. Somewhere, in the distant reaches of her mind, unease made its presence felt.

'Eighty per cent?' she asked.

'Yes,' said Phuti. 'And she had very good references too.'

'And her name?' asked Mma Makutsi.

Phuti spoke evenly, obviously unaware of the explosive potential of the information he was about to reveal. 'Violet Sephotho,' he said. 'I believe that you know her. She said that she had been at the Botswana Secretarial College with you. She said that you had been good friends.'

Mma Makutsi found it difficult to pour the boiling water into the teapot. Her right hand, normally so steady, was shaking now and she had to use her other hand to come to its assistance.

Violet Sephotho! Eighty per cent!

She succeeded in filling the teapot but only at the cost of several small spillages of hot water, one of which was upon her wrist, and stung.

'You have spilled hot water?'

She brushed the incident aside. 'Nothing. I am fine.' But she was thinking. Eighty per cent? That was a lie, of course, as Violet had rarely achieved much more than fifty per cent in any of the examinations at the college. Indeed, Mma Makutsi could remember an occasion when Violet had not attended one of the examinations and had pleaded ill health, even producing, in class the next day, what purported to be a doctor's letter to back up her claim. 'Anyone can write a letter,' one of Mma Makutsi's friends had whispered, loud enough for Violet Sephotho to hear and spin round to glare at her accusers. She had stared at the wrong person, at Mma Makutsi, and at that moment an abiding hostility, fuelled by envy, had begun.

Mma Makutsi already knew the answer to her question and so did not really need to ask it. But she had to. 'You took her then?' she said. 'That Violet Seph . . .' She could not bring herself to utter the name in its entirety, and her voice trailed away.

'Of course,' said Phuti. He looked surprised that she could have thought any other outcome was possible. Eighty per cent might not have been ninety-seven per cent, but it was still eighty per cent.

'I see.'

She looked away. Should she tell him? 'I am not sure that she got eighty per cent,' she said. She tried to make her voice sound even, but it did not,

53

and she thought that he would be able to tell that something was wrong.

'But she did,' said Phuti. 'She told me. Eighty per cent.'

Mma Makutsi wanted to say, 'But she is a liar, Phuti! Can you not tell? She is a very big liar.' She could not say that, though, because Phuti was a fair-minded man and would ask, even if mildly, for proof, which would be difficult to furnish. So instead she said, 'Why do you think she wants to work in the shop? If she is so highly qualified, why does she not want to get a job in some big firm? A job with the diamond company, for instance?'

Phuti shrugged. 'It is not always that easy to get a job with the diamond people,' he said. 'There are people lining up for those jobs. And anyway, it is a well-paid post, this. There are many benefits.'

Indeed there are, thought Mma Makutsi. And she was sure that one of the benefits, at least from Violet Sephotho's perspective, was that of working closely with Phuti, who was very comfortably off, not only with his share of the Double Comfort Furniture Shop, that would become a full interest once his aged father died, but also with his large herd of cattle at the Radiphuti cattle post. There could be no doubt, none at all, that Violet's real motive in seeking the job was to prise Phuti away from his lawful fiancée—Grace Makutsi, assistant detective—and guide him into her own, wicked, calculating, waiting arms. Oh, it was clear enough, but there would be no point in spelling this out to Phuti because he simply would not see it. Nor, she thought, would he react well to being warned about Violet; shortly after she had become engaged, Mma Ramotswe had told her to be careful about telling one's fiancé what to do. 'Men do not like it,' she said. 'You must never make a man feel that he is being told what to do. He will run away. I have seen that happen so many times.'

She served Phuti his cup of tea and they sat together at the table. She thought that Phuti had no idea of her concern, as he chatted away about other furniture matters. There was a new type of table, he said, that could be folded up and stored under a bed.

'That is very useful,' he said. 'I think that there will be many people who will want to keep a table under their bed.' Mma Makutsi was non-committal; there may be many such people, but this was not the time to think about them. This was a time to think about that scheming Violet Sephotho and what could be done about her. She could try to warn her off, Mma Makutsi thought, by telling her that she was well aware of what her real intentions were. Violet, however, was not the sort to buckle under a threat; she would simply deny that she knew what the accusation was about. Another option would be to speak to Phuti's uncles. That was always an option in Botswana, where uncles on both sides took a close interest in engagements and marriages. It would be perfectly proper for her uncles to go to see Phuti's uncles and to express their concern about the danger that Violet represented to the future marriage.

Yet there was a difficulty here: this would have been a reasonable course of action, but only if she could trust her uncles to be discreet, and she feared that she could not do that. Her senior uncle, in particular, the one with the broken nose, was noted for his lack of tact. He would insist on being

55

involved in any negotiation and he would be bound to make matters worse. He would make demands, possibly even threats, and a family like the Radiphuti family, that spoke quietly and with circumspection, would be offended if her uncle made too much fuss. Oh, I am miserable, thought Mma Makutsi. I am stuck and miserable like a cow on a railway line who sees the train from Mafikeng bearing down upon her and cannot bring herself to move.

CHAPTER FIVE

THERE IS PLENTY OF WORK FOR LOVE TO DO

There was no question the next morning of Mma Ramotswe's being able to make the journey into the office by foot. It was difficult enough, in fact, for her to walk to the bathroom without limping when she got out of bed shortly before six o'clock, such was the discomfort of the blister on her right foot. The plaster that Dr Moffat had put on the day before had peeled off during the night, leaving the angry skin uncovered. That could be remedied, of course: she kept a supply of plasters in the bathroom cupboard, mainly for Puso, who was always scratching himself on thorns and nails and other things that lay in wait for passing boys. At least he had not broken anything, unlike his friend at school, an appealing boy with a wide smile, who was always appearing with an arm in a sling or an ankle in plaster. That boy fell from trees, Puso

56

explained. 'He is always climbing, Mma, and then he falls down and breaks when he hits the ground. He does not mind, though. He is a very brave boy and he will join the Botswana Defence Force when he is twelve, I think.'

Mma Ramotswe laughed. 'You cannot join the Botswana Defence Force when you are twelve,' she said. 'You have to be much older. Eighteen, I think. Something like that. And being a soldier is not just a matter of climbing trees.'

'It helps, though, doesn't it?' argued Puso. 'If you can climb trees, you can hide when you see the enemy coming.'

Mma Ramotswe shook a finger in mock disapproval. 'I do not think that is what a brave soldier is meant to do, Puso.' She paused. He had said *when you see the enemy coming*. But Botswana had no enemies, a fact which was a source of both relief—who would want enemies?—and pride. Her country had never been aggressive, had never espoused violence, had never taken sides in the squabbles of others. She wondered how people could sleep if they knew that somebody, in their name, was dropping bombs on other people or breaking into their homes and taking them away somewhere. Why did they do it? Why was it necessary to kill and maim other people when the other people would be just the same as yourself— people who wanted to live with their families and go to work in the morning and have enough to eat at the end of the day? That was not much to ask of the world, even if for many the world could not grant even that small request.

The contemplation of the greater suffering of the world, though, did not stop one's own small

57

blister from hurting, and Mma Ramotswe's right foot now throbbed painfully as she lifted it on to the edge of the bath. She looked at the site of the pain, touching the skin gently, as one might touch the branch of a thorny acacia. The skin felt hot and was taut as a drum where fluid had built up underneath. She wondered whether she should take a needle to the tiny bubble and burst it, releasing the pressure and easing the pain. But she had always been taught to leave the body to sort itself out, to absorb or expel according to its own moods, its own timetable of recovery. So she simply applied another plaster, which seemed to help, and went down the corridor to make her morning cup of redbush tea.

Mr J. L. B. Matekoni was still asleep. Mma Ramotswe was always the first to arise in the morning, and she enjoyed the brief private time before the others would get up and start making demands of her. There would be breakfast to prepare, children's clothes to find, husband's clothes to find too; there would be a hundred things to do. But that lay half an hour or so ahead; for the time being she could be alone in her garden, as the sun came up over the border to the east, beyond Tlokweng, hovering over the horizon like a floating ball of fire. There was no finer time of day than this, she thought, when the air was cool and when, amidst the lower branches of the trees, there was still a hint, just the merest hint, of translucent white mist.

She looked past her vegetable garden, her poor, struggling vegetable garden, to the house itself. That building, she thought, contains my people; under that roof are the two foster-children,

58

Motholeli and Puso, and Mr J. L. B. Matekoni, my husband. And, parked outside the kitchen, to complete her world, was her tiny white van, still there but not necessarily for ever. She took a sip of her tea. Nothing was for ever; not her, not Mr J. L. B. Matekoni, not the house, not even Botswana. She had recently read that scientists could work out exactly when everything would come to an end and the earth would be swallowed up by the sun—or was it by some other planet?— and there would be nothing left of any of us. That had made her think, and she had raised the issue with her friend, Bishop Trevor Mwamba, over tea outside the Anglican Cathedral, one Sunday morning after the seven thirty service in English and just before the nine thirty service in Setswana. 'Is it true,' she had asked, 'that the sun will swallow up the earth and that will be that?'

Trevor had smiled. 'I do not think that this is going to happen in the near future, Mma Ramotswe,' he had replied. 'Certainly not by next Tuesday, when the Botswana Mothers' Union meets. And, frankly, I don't think that we should worry too much about that. Our concern should be what is happening right now. There is plenty of work for love to do, you know.'

There is plenty of work for love to do. That was a wonderful way of putting it, and she had told him that this could be the best possible motto for anybody to have.

She finished her tea and began to walk back into the house. *There is plenty of work for love to do*. Yes. There was breakfast to be made, and letters to be answered, and the problems in clients' lives to be sorted out. There was quite enough to do without

59

worrying about the sun consuming the earth. Yes, one should not worry too much, but then she looked at her van and thought: how long will I be able to keep you going? One more day? One more week? And then how are we going to say goodbye, after so many years? It would be like losing a best friend, a faithful companion—it would be every bit as hard as that.

Mma Ramotswe had an anxious moment when she turned the key in the van's ignition that morning, but it was an anxious moment that lasted just that—a moment. Obediently, and without making any suspicious noise, the engine started and she began to drive off slowly. She breathed a sigh of relief; perhaps the problem really had been temporary—no more, as she had previously considered, than some piece of grit in the cogs that made up the gearbox or the . . . she could not think of the name of any of the other moving parts, but she knew that there were levers and springs and things that went up and down; any of those could have been half-stuck. But as she began to drive down Zebra Drive, taking great care not to go too fast, the van resumed its protests. There was what sounded like a hiccup, and then the loud blast of a backfire, and following hard on that there was the familiar knocking sound. Her heart sank. The tiny white van was dying.

But just as soon as she reached this bleak conclusion, a way out presented itself to her. She would follow Dr Moffat's advice. Fanwell, the younger of the two apprentices, was approachable and knew how to keep a secret. She would ask him to look at the van after work. She would drive him back to his house and he could have a look at it there. Neither Mr J. L. B. Matekoni, nor Charlie, need ever know about this visit, and if Fanwell could deal with the problem then nobody need ever be any the wiser.

She had her chance to speak to the apprentice later that morning.

'I'm going to stretch my legs,' she said to Mma Makutsi. 'I have been sitting down for too long.'

Mma Makutsi looked up from a letter she was reading. 'That is a very good idea, Mma. If you do not stretch your legs, the blood sinks down to the feet and there is not enough for the brain. That is why some people are so stupid. They are the ones who have too much blood in their feet.'

Mma Ramotswe stared at her assistant. 'That is an interesting theory, Mma. But I am not sure that it is quite true. I know some very clever people who sit down all the time. Look at them up at the University of Botswana. They spend most of the time sitting down, but they are very clever. They clearly have enough blood for their brains. No, Mma, I don't think that has anything to do with it.'

Mma Makutsi had pouted. 'You should not argue with science, Mma,' she muttered. 'Many people have made that mistake.' It had looked for a moment as if she was going to say something else, but she did not. So Mma Ramotswe left the office and made her way round to the front of the garage.

The two apprentices were standing underneath a car that had been raised for inspection. Charlie was pointing at something with a screwdriver and Fanwell was peering up into the undercarriage of the car, a region of pipes and cables not unlike the intestines of a living creature, and as vulnerable,

61

she thought with a shudder.

Fanwell turned to look at Mma Ramotswe, and she beckoned him discreetly to join her.

'Will you come for a little walk with me?' she said. 'Charlie can take care of that car.' It would be a short walk, she thought, as she still had her blister, even though it had stopped throbbing.

Fanwell glanced over to Charlie, who nodded to him. Mma Ramotswe occasionally asked the apprentices to run errands for her, and he imagined that this was what she wanted of him.

They walked away from the garage towards the piece of scrubland that lay immediately behind the building. This was the edge of the town, half bush, half suburb, where cattle sometimes wandered, bringing with them their sounds of the true countryside, the sound of cattle bells. Here hornbills might perch on branches and contemplate the bustle of the Tlokweng Road before flying away again, in long swooping curves that led from tree to tree. Here small gusts of wind, the sort of wind that came from nowhere in particular, might briefly blow scraps of paper or the occasional plastic bag, lifting these bits of detritus half-heartedly before dropping them again and moving on. Here paths would begin and lead off into the deeper bush before disappearing altogether at the foot of the hills to the south of the town.

'I wanted to talk to you, Fanwell,' said Mma Ramotswe. 'I wanted to ask you a favour.'

The young man looked at her nervously and then glanced over his shoulder in the direction of the garage. He was not as confident as the older apprentice and he usually relied on Charlie to answer for both of them.

'Don't worry,' soothed Mma Ramotswe. 'It's not a big favour. Or, maybe it is a bit big. Not too big, but a bit big.'

'I will always help you, Mma,' said Fanwell uncertainly. 'You can ask me. I will do my best.'

Mma Ramotswe touched him gently on the forearm. 'Thank you, Fanwell. It is my van. I need you to look at my van.'

They stopped walking. The apprentice looked at her in puzzlement. 'Your van?'

'My van is very ill,' said Mma Ramotswe. 'There is something very badly wrong with it.'

Fanwell thought for a moment. 'Have you spoken to Mr J. L. B. Matekoni about it? He is the man, Mma. There is nothing that he cannot fix.'

Mma Ramotswe sighed. He was right to say that there was nothing that Mr J. L. B. Matekoni could not fix, but that was not the same thing as saying that there was nothing that he *would* not fix. There comes a time in the life of machinery, Mr J. L. B. Matekoni was fond of saying, when it is right to say goodbye. That had happened eventually with the water pump at the orphan farm; he had insisted that he could no longer fix the ancient machine, dating back to the days of the Bechuanaland Protectorate. Mma Ramotswe was in no doubt that this is what he thought of the tiny white van. In his view, its time had clearly come.

She explained the difficulty to Fanwell. 'So,' she said, 'if I am to keep my van, then I must have it fixed by somebody else. Mr J. L. B. Matekoni would just get rid of it.'

'But he would see me,' the apprentice protested. 'If I took your van into the garage he would see it and know what I was doing.'

'Of course he would,' said Mma Ramotswe. 'That's why I would like you to take a look at it at home. At your place.'

Fanwell frowned. 'But I haven't got the tools I need there. I haven't got an inspection pit. There is nothing.'

'Just look at it,' pleaded Mma Ramotswe. 'Could you not just look at it? You wouldn't need many tools for that. A few spanners maybe. Nothing more.'

Fanwell scratched his head. 'I don't know, Mma. I don't know . . .'

'I could drive you home,' said Mma Ramotswe. 'Then you could look at it and let me know what you think. Maybe it is just a small thing, which you could fix very easily. I will pay you, of course.'

Fanwell hesitated. He was notoriously impecunious and the prospect of a bit of pin money was very attractive. 'Maybe,' he said. 'Maybe I could look. I can't guarantee anything, though, Mma.'

'None of us can guarantee anything, Fanwell,' said Mma Ramotswe. 'Not even that the sun will come up tomorrow.'

Fanwell smiled. 'Would you like to bet on that one, Mma Ramotswe?' he asked. 'Ten pula?'

*   *   *

When the time came to leave the office that evening, Mr J. L. B. Matekoni was out on a call, and so there was no need for discretion.

'I am going to drive Fanwell back to his place,' Mma Ramotswe announced to Mma Makutsi. 'I

64

can drop you off first, Mma, and then go on to Old Naledi, where he lives.'

'And what about me?' asked Charlie, who had overheard the conversation from outside the door. 'Why are you taking him and not me, Mma? What is wrong with me?'

'There is a lot wrong with you, Charlie,' interjected Mma Makutsi. 'I have been making a big list these last few years and it is now about three pages long.'

'I was talking to Mma Ramotswe,' Charlie called out. 'I was talking to the lady who is the boss. It is best to talk to the man who is selling the cow and not to the cow itself.'

Mma Makutsi's eyes flashed in anger. 'Are you calling me a cow, Charlie? Did I hear you right? Are you saying that I am a cow?' She turned to Mma Ramotswe in outrage. 'Did you hear that, Mma? Did you hear what he said?'

Mma Ramotswe made a placatory gesture. 'I do not think you two should fight. And you must not say things like that, Charlie. It is very rude to call another person a chicken.'

'A chicken? I did not call her a chicken. I called her a . . .'

'Well, there you are,' said Mma Ramotswe. 'You've admitted it.'

Charlie was silent.

'And I'll drive you home some time next week. I promise you. It will be your turn then. Now it is Fanwell's.'

They closed up the office and walked over to the tiny white van. The blister had stopped troubling her; it had burst, she thought, and walking was comfortable again. If only all our troubles were like that; and perhaps they were. Perhaps the trick was to do what was necessary to deal with them, to put a plaster on them and then forget that they were there.

Mma Makutsi got into the passenger seat while Fanwell climbed into the back. Then, as they set off, Mma Makutsi launched into a description of what she was planning to cook for Phuti Radiphuti that evening. She would make a stew, she said, which had the best Botswana beef in it, the very best. She had been given the meat by a cousin who had slaughtered it himself and who said that he knew the parents and the grandparents of the animal in question. 'And they were all delicious, he said, Mma. He said that they were a very delicious family.'

Mma Ramotswe dropped Mma Makutsi off at her house and Fanwell came to take her place in the passenger seat. As they drove off, he listened very carefully to the engine note, frowning in concentration as Mma Ramotswe took the van up to the speed at which the noise became noticeable.

'That is a very bad sound, Mma,' he said. 'Very bad.'

Mma Ramotswe had been expecting this verdict, but she urged him not to make up his mind before he had actually looked at the engine. 'It could be a temporary noise,' she ventured. 'Don't you think that it could be a temporary noise, Fanwell?'

He did not. 'It is permanent,' he said. 'That is a very permanent noise, Mma Ramotswe.'

They turned off the main road and began to travel into the heart of Old Naledi, the sprawling collection of meagre houses, some not much better than shelters, that stood cheek by jowl with the rest of well-set Gaborone. By the standards of African shanty towns elsewhere it was princely, with standpipes for fresh water and lighting along the bumpy roads, but it was still the most deprived part of town and if one was looking for poverty in an otherwise prosperous country, then this was the place to find it.

CHAPTER SIX

FANWELL'S HOUSE

It was not the smallest of houses, as it had two rooms; there were smaller places near by—single-roomed, made of baked-mud bricks and topped with slanting roofs of corrugated iron, kept standing not so much by the builder's art but by gravity and hope. Fanwell's house stood at the intersection of two unpaved roads in the middle of Old Naledi, surrounded by a tiny yard at the back of which stood a lean-to privy and a couple of small thorn trees. The front door, which gave more or less directly on to the road, was painted bright blue, the national colour, a sign of pride. And although the yard was meagre and the surroundings bleak, the whole place had a tended air about it, the look of having been swept, dusted perhaps by some house-proud hand.

They arrived at that time of the day when late afternoon imperceptibly becomes early evening, a time of lengthening shadows and softening light. There would still be a good hour before darkness descended, and Mma Ramotswe hoped that this would give the apprentice time enough to examine the van. She would sit under one of the trees, she thought, while he worked; there was a comfortable-looking stone there that was obviously used for just such purposes. That would be where the owner of the house sat, she thought; well, she was Fanwell's guest and could sit there if invited.

'So this is your place, Fanwell,' she said as she negotiated the van off the road and on to the small patch of yard.

He turned and smiled at her proudly. 'Yes, this is my place, Mma. Or rather it is my grandmother's place. I live here, you see. I live here with the others.'

Mma Ramotswe nodded. It was not unusual for a grandmother to be the head of a household, especially now, with that illness that had stalked the land. But who, she wondered, were the others? They could be anybody: Fanwell's brothers and sisters, his cousins, even uncles and aunts. It did not really matter what the relationship was; a home was a home whoever lived in it, it was the same family no matter how attenuated the links of blood and lineage.

She parked the van carefully beside a large tin tub turned upside down in the yard. That would be the family bath. As she switched off the engine and opened her door, the front door of the house opened and a child of about ten peered out. Fanwell gestured to the child, who stepped out shyly, followed by a smaller child, a boy, and then another boy.

Mma Ramotswe smiled at the girl. 'How are you, little one?'

The child lowered her eyes, as was respectful. 'I

am very well, Mma.'

Mma Ramotswe reached out and took her hand. It felt strangely dry, as the hands of children sometimes can. 'And these are your brothers?'

The child nodded and then pointed to the smaller boy. 'That one is my brother by another mother.'

The door opened and another girl came out— this one rather older, thirteen, perhaps, or fourteen. Mma Ramotswe noticed the early signs of womanhood and thought: if only she could be protected. But how could one do that in the absence of a mother and a father? She looked away. Somehow humanity got by; somehow children grew up in the most unpromising of surroundings, as in this cramped little house in this clutter of lanes and paths and tumbledown dwellings. And many of them, against all the odds, made something of their lives, studying by candlelight or by electric light dangerously stolen from the mains outside, poring over the books that could lead them out of this and into something better. Fanwell had done it: he must have had to battle to get the school certificate that meant that he could start a mechanics' apprenticeship. And if it had not been for Charlie, who had distracted him and led him astray, he would have completed the apprenticeship by now and would be earning enough, perhaps, to escape Old Naledi altogether.

Fanwell turned to the teenage girl. 'Take the aunty into the house and make her some tea,' he said. 'The aunty likes tea.'

The girl nodded and gestured for Mma Ramotswe to follow her.

'My grandmother will be back soon,' said

Fanwell. 'She will also look after you, Mma. In the meantime, I'll start on your van.'

Mma Ramotswe followed the girl into the house and found herself in a small, square room. At the far end, behind a tattered blue curtain, a doorway led into the back room, the sleeping quarters, she imagined. The front room, dimly lit by daylight admitted through a single window, was cluttered with the family's possessions: a tin trunk from which the clasp had fallen away, a table of varnished yellow wood, straight-backed chairs, an open cupboard with tins of food and cooking implements stacked on the shelves. Against the wall opposite the window stood a small electric stove—two hot plates and a tiny, rickety oven. This was home to . . . Mma Ramotswe thought: five young people, if one included Fanwell, and one grandmother. And she saw that there were six white enamel plates stacked on one of the shelves; six single plates on which all the family's food was served.

The girl produced a simple kettle from somewhere. It was already filled with water and she placed it delicately on the stove.

'It will not be long, Mma.'

Mma Ramotswe smiled at her. The smaller children, the girl and the two boys, had sidled into the room and were standing near the window, watching her.

'Shall I sit down here?' asked Mma Ramotswe, indicating one of the chairs.

The girl nodded. 'That is my grandmother's chair, Mma,' she said. 'But she will not mind. She can sit on one of the others.'

Mma Ramotswe looked at the other children. It

70

was difficult to tell with certainty, but two of them looked very alike; the others were different. Brothers and sisters by other mothers, she thought. Of course, that applied to all of us, did it not? We were all brothers and sisters by different mothers.

She turned to the teenage girl. 'Do you go to school?'

The girl nodded. 'I am in Form Two.' There was a gravity about the way she spoke, her answers being delivered with precision and only after what seemed like a pause for consideration.

'And what is your best subject?' asked Mma Ramotswe. 'Let me guess? You are good at English. Am I right?'

The girl's eyes widened. 'How could you tell, Mma? Yes, that is my best subject.'

Mma Ramotswe chuckled. 'I am a detective, you see. I know how to find clues. And there are many clues in this place. I saw those two books on the shelf there. Those ones. An English dictionary and a book of stories. I thought: there is somebody in this house who is a keen reader. I could tell that. And those ones over there,' she nodded in the direction of the smaller children, 'they are too small to be reading English dictionaries. And Fanwell . . . Well, he is a young man, and they do not read dictionaries either. So that meant Grandmother or you, and I decided that it must be you.'

The girl smiled. It was the first time that she had smiled, and Mma Ramotswe saw her face light up. 'Fanwell told me that you were a detective, Mma,' the girl said. 'He told me that you are a very clever lady.' She paused. 'And he also said that he often helps you solve cases.'

Mma Ramotswe gave nothing away. 'Of course he does,' she said. 'Your brother is very useful.'

The kettle had now begun to boil and the girl busied herself with the making of tea. The brew was thin and the milk powdered, but Mma Ramotswe was thirsty and it was welcome. As she began to sip the tea, the front door opened and the grandmother came in.

*   *   *

They sat together at the table, Fanwell's grandmother and Mma Ramotswe. The teenage girl who had made the tea and the younger children had been sent outside, while the grandmother and her visitor talked.

'I am from Thamaga,' said the old woman. 'I was born there, the firstborn of my parents. Number one of seven. Three girls and four boys. There are three of us left, Mma, after all these years. Three.'

'You are still here,' said Mma Ramotswe. 'That is a good thing.'

The grandmother acknowledged the truth of what Mma Ramotswe said. 'Yes, it is. But then when you are old like me, you think that the whole world is changing. There are new people everywhere. New buildings. And all this rush— everybody is in a hurry. And you sit there and think: why is everybody in a hurry? That will not make the crops grow any quicker, will it? It will not.

'Thamaga is a good place and I was very happy there. I went to school and I was good at the things that they taught us. I can write, Mma. I can read

72

too. I am not an illiterate. I have a bible in the bedroom that I know a lot of by heart. I have read it many times. I can say much of it without reading. "In the beginning . . ."'

Mma Ramotswe nodded. 'Yes, I have heard that.' And added, quickly, 'Tell me what happened to you, Mma. Out in Thamaga. What happened?'

The old woman looked at her in surprise. Her eyes, Mma Ramotswe noticed, were unusually moist round the edges, as are the eyes of one who has looked too long into the smoke of a wood fire, smarting. 'Nothing happened to me in Thamaga, Mma. Nothing.'

Mma Ramotswe smiled. 'In all those years, Mma?'

The old woman's face creased with amusement. 'I suppose that things happened. It's just that when you are living in a village, it seems at the time that there is nothing happening. You know how it is. There is the hot season. Then there are the rains. Then it gets cold. And then the hot weather starts again.

'And children are born,' she went on, 'and they grow up and go away and more children are born. That is what happens in a place like Thamaga.'

Mma Ramotswe knew what she meant. It had been the same in Mochudi when she was a girl. Something had happened in her life because she had come to Gaborone and started the No. 1 Ladies' Detective Agency, but there were those who had stayed. Nothing much had happened in their lives, and yet were they unhappier for that? She did not think so.

'I was married when I was sixteen,' said the old woman. 'I did not really want to get married

73

because I would have liked to have been a nurse, or an assistant to a nurse. They took girls at the Scottish hospital in Molepolole, the Livingstone Hospital. You know the place, Mma?'

'I know it,' said Mma Ramotswe. 'Dr Merriweather's hospital. When he was there. He is late now, but people still love him. Late people are still loved, aren't they, Mma?'

'Yes, they are. You are right. And that is the place. I could have gone there and they would have trained me, but my senior uncle was against it. He said that if I became a nurse I would go and work in South Africa and never come back, and then who would look after him and the others? So they made me marry. I think that they were interested in the cattle they would get for me, too. In the *lobola*.

'There was a young man who was the nephew of a friend of my senior uncle—my own father was late, you see. So they introduced us—they brought this young man to the house and they sat and watched as we talked. The young man was very shy and he could not talk about anything. He looked at me as if he was trying to say, *Sorry, this is not my idea*. When he looked at me in that way, I knew that I would be able to love him. I did not like men who never thought about how a woman was feeling. This one was thinking of me. So I said to my senior uncle that he had found a very good young man and that I would behave as a good wife should and he should not worry that they would ask for their cattle back. That is what my uncle was really worried about, Mma.

'We were married and then almost straight away my husband went off and got a job in Gaborone as

74

a government driver. They were looking for drivers then as the Government had just found diamonds and they had money to spend on cars. They bought many cars with the diamond money and they needed men to drive them.

'He was very popular with the government people and they made him a Driver Class One. This meant that he could drive big government cars and not just the cars of small officials. Now and then he drove Seretse Khama himself, Mma, and then he also sometimes drove President Masire if the President's own driver was not well. President Masire used to like to talk to him about ostriches because he was very interested in them— the President was—and my husband knew something about ostriches. He did not like ostriches very much but he never told the President that. That would have been rude, Mma.

'While he was doing all this driving for the Government, Mma, I stayed behind in Thamaga and brought up the children. We had two sons and two daughters. One of them was the mother of Fanwell. She is late now. The other girl is married to a man on that side'—she pointed in the direction of the border—'and we do not see her very much. There is something wrong, I think, but she will not say what it is. She is not happy, Mma. One of the boys went to Maun and worked in one of those places up there. He became late, and so did his wife. That meant that their children came to me. The other one went to Francistown. He is a clerk, a very important clerk, but he does not send us any money, Mma. Not one thebe.

'While I was staying in the village with my own children, all those years ago, my husband found another woman in Gaborone. I knew about that, Mma, but I said nothing. Some of my friends said to me that I should go and find that woman and poison her, but I said no, I would not do that. I have never poisoned anybody, Mma, and I would not poison even this bad woman who was seeing my husband and taking him away from me. Have you ever poisoned anybody, Mma? I do not think you have! When I see you I do not think: *That is a poisoner.* I do not think that, Mma.

'And then, Mma, after many years in Gaborone, my husband became late. And that is when I found out that he had had a child by this other woman, and that child, when she was fifteen, had her own child, who is one of those smaller children you have met here. And then she had another one. They are the granddaughters of that bad woman. Their own mother just went away. She left the girls with some neighbours and told them to get in touch with me because she had heard that I was the grandmother.

'So I had to come to Gaborone and sort out all these grandchildren who had nobody to look after them. I found this place, Mma—which may be small but is very comfortable. There is enough room for all of us if we are careful how we move about and do not bump into one another too much.

'When I was in Thamaga, Mma, I earned some money as a potter. You know that they have a pottery out there? You have seen their work, maybe. I was one of the ladies who made pots, very good pots, Mma. So when I came to Gaborone I thought that I could make some pots and sell them out at that shop, Botswanacraft; you may have seen it, Mma. They are kind people there, and they are very happy to take your work if they can sell it. They take some of my pots, but not too many, and I only carn a few pula from each one. Who wants Botswana pots these days, Mma, when there are so many other things for people to buy? And it is also hard to get the right dye here in Gaborone, Mma. Out there in Thamaga we had all the things that we needed—we just had to go and find them. We had good clay. We had many fine dyes from red earth and from plants that we knew. All of that was just given to us by God, and we did not have to pay for it. Here in Gaborone, there is nothing that is free, even the things that God gives to Botswana. Somebody comes along and puts a price on them. Then they say, *No, that is twenty pula that one, and that one is fifty,* and so on. One day they are going to put a price on the air itself, Mma, and say, *No, you cannot breathe unless you give us forty pula for the air. Do you think air is free?'*

She became silent. Mma Ramotswe looked into her eyes. The whites were a strange colour, slightly ochre perhaps; burst blood vessels, perhaps, a long time ago; rust; the dust of many years. Any of these could be the explanation.

The old woman drew breath. 'Fanwell is such a good boy,' she said. 'He works very hard in the garage and do you know something, Mma? Every pay-day he gives me all the money he gets from Mr J. L. B. Matekoni. Every pula. That is how we live, Mma—all of us. It is only Fanwell's money that we have, and the few pula that I make from my pots. That is what keeps us, Mma. All of us.'

Mma Ramotswe sat quite still. *All of us.* Until you hear the whole story, until you dig deeper, and listen, she thought, you know only a tiny part of the goodness of the human heart.

CHAPTER SEVEN

PUSO MEETS ROPS THOBEGA, BIG HERO

Of course it was not good news that Mma Ramotswe received from Fanwell. But the next day was Saturday, and she put the whole matter out of her mind for the time being. The tiny white van was still working—just—and as long as she crawled along, the protests from the engine were not too loud. So she did not change her plans for that day, which, unusually for a Saturday, involved a work engagement, and a most unusual one at that.

The previous morning, Mma Ramotswe had received a telephone call from her new client, Mr Leungo Molofololo.

'When are you going to start working on my case, Mma Ramotswe?' the businessman had asked.

'Very soon, Rra,' said Mma Ramotswe, glancing at Mma Makutsi as she spoke. The glance had a meaning for her assistant, who immediately inserted a piece of paper into her typewriter and began typing noisily.

'As you can probably hear, Rra,' she said, 'the office is rather busy at the moment. But I shall start on your case as soon as I can.'

It was a genuine excuse; Mma Ramotswe had been busy, but she never expected clients to understand that. She knew how special each of us is to ourselves, and how inconceivable it is to us that somebody else's concerns should be more pressing than our own. And the richer people were, she had noticed, the more difficult it became for them to understand that there were other people with hopes and plans of their own, however small these might seem from the heights occupied by rich people. Perhaps to them we look like ants, thought Mma Ramotswe; and she imagined, for a moment, a rich person looking down and saying, *That ant there, that traditionally built ant, is Mma Ramotswe. And that one scurrying around over there, that ant with big glasses, is Mma Makutsi.*

Mr Molofololo, though, proved not to be like that. He said that he understood that she was busy and that his matter would have to take its place in the queue. To which Mma Ramotswe replied, 'It is a very small queue, Rra, and your case is near the top of the list now.'

'In that case, Mma Ramotswe,' said Mr Molofololo, 'I hope that you will be able to come with me to a football match tomorrow. We are playing a big, important game at the Stadium, and a great deal is at stake.'

Mma Ramotswe thought quickly. Her Saturdays were something of a ritual. She always went to the President Hotel for tea in the morning, and then, after a quick shopping trip, she would return and make lunch. In the afternoon she would have a nap, as Mr J. L. B. Matekoni also sometimes did, before getting up to make biscuits for tea. It was a very satisfactory way of spending a Saturday, and the prospect of attending a football match did not strike her as being very attractive. On the other hand, Puso might come too; he was always talking about soccer, although she never paid much attention to what he said about it. Many of the things that boys and men said were like that, she felt; important enough to them, but not all that important to girls and women.

'I will come to the match, Rra,' she said and then, thinking quickly, she added, 'Would you be able to send a car to collect me? My own van is . . . is temporarily out of order.'

'I shall get my driver to collect you at two o'clock,' said Mr Molofololo.

'And my foster-son?' said Mma Ramotswe. 'May he come too?'

'You will both be the guests of Mr Leungo Molofololo,' said Mr Molofololo. 'Guaranteed.'

Mma Ramotswe thanked him and gave him directions to the house. Then, before they said goodbye, she asked what he thought were the prospects for the match. There was hesitation at the other end of the line; just that silence that, on the telephone, always signals, *I am thinking*. Eventually he answered. 'The game will be stolen from us, Mma,' he said. 'Everybody knows that we are the stronger team. But the game will be stolen.'

There was only one word for what Mma Ramotswe heard in his voice, and that was *sorrow*. And as she rang off, she said to Mma Makutsi, 'Mma, have you noticed how things that are really not very important can become very important? A football match? What is it? A game. But to men it is the beginning and end of the world.'

'Not to all men,' said Mma Makutsi primly. 'Phuti Radiphuti has no time for football. He says that it is just a waste of time.'

Mma Ramotswe smiled. 'But surely Phuti has

80

something that is important to him,' she said, adding quickly, 'Apart from you, Mma. You are very important to him.'

Mma Makutsi acknowledged the compliment. 'Phuti likes collecting model aeroplanes,' she said. 'That is important to him.'

Mma Ramotswe suppressed a smile. 'That must be very interesting,' she said. 'There are not many men, I think, who do that.'

'Oh there are, Mma,' said Mma Makutsi. 'There are four other men in Gaborone who are interested in model aeroplanes; actually, three of them are still boys. They come to Phuti's house and show each other their planes. They enjoy that very much.'

'Everybody needs a hobby,' said Mma Ramotswe. 'Particularly men. They need hobbies because they do not have enough to do. We women always have too much to do and do not have to spend our time watching football or playing with . . . collecting model aeroplanes.'

'You are right, Mma,' said Mma Makutsi. 'The whole world is on the shoulders of women. How does that song go? Do you remember that song?'

Mma Ramotswe did, and she sang a snatch of it then and there, improvising the words, which were all about how one is on the shoulders of the other but that there is no pain in this, and nobody would have it otherwise.

*   *   *

'The Kalahari Swoopers?' asked Puso. 'Are you sure, Mma?'

The small boy's reaction—something between

81

incredulity and sheer delight—had not surprised Mma Ramotswe when she told him that they were to be the guests of no less a person than the owner of the team.

'His driver will pick us up,' she said. 'So I want you to have a bath beforehand and put on your best shirt—the red one, I think—so that you will be smart when you meet the captain.'

This news was almost too much for Puso to absorb. The captain of the Kalahari Swoopers, Rops Thobega, was something of a hero. Even Mma Ramotswe, who knew nothing about football, had heard all about Rops Thobega and his doings. He was one of the more senior players in Botswana football, having been a professional player since his late teens. Now, at the age of thirty, he was getting to the point where younger men were breathing down his neck, but he was still one of the most popular and appreciated of players, and recently had even been praised in Parliament for his initiatives with delinquent youths. 'No boy behaves badly if he spends enough time on the football pitch,' he was quoted as saying. 'Give me a young man who is coming up before the courts and I will change him.'

A vain promise, some said, but it had been one that he had delivered upon. In particular, he had turned round three young men who had been facing jail and who had become strong football players. Now all three of them were in a team— admittedly a weak team, but they had given up on their bad behaviour.

'Rops Thobega?' asked Puso breathlessly. 'Will I meet him, Mma?'

'I think there is a good chance,' said Mma

Ramotswe. 'We are the guests of Mr Leungo Molofololo and he said something about introducing us to the players.'

'That is very exciting, Mma,' said Puso. 'I will take my football and ask him to sign it.'

Such was his excitement that Puso was ready a full two hours before Mr Molofololo's driver was due to collect them. Then, in the comfort of the large Mercedes-Benz that had been sent by Mr Molofololo, they drove the short distance to the Stadium. It was a hot afternoon, and it would have been preferable to have the windows of the car closed in order to allow the cooling system to operate, but Puso insisted on opening his so that passers-by could see him sitting in the car. Mma Ramotswe smiled. She was pleased to see the boy get such a thrill from the outing.

They were greeted at the Stadium by one of Mr Molofololo's officials, who led them into a room at the back of the seating area. There they found Mr Molofololo and, sitting opposite, wearing football shorts and shirt, Rops Thobega himself. Mr Molofololo glanced up when Mma Ramotswe entered and he gestured for her to take the vacant seat beside him.

'Rops and I always have a talk before a game,' Mr Molofololo said after the introductions had been made. 'We talk about strategy.'

'I should not interrupt you,' said Mma Ramotswe, glancing at Puso, who was standing at her side, staring intently at Rops. 'There is a young man here . . .'

Rops looked at Puso and smiled. 'Who wants me to sign his football?'

Puso stepped forward, holding the ball out to

83

Rops, who took it and signed. 'Work hard at school, young man,' the great football player said. 'Play football. Eat healthily. Be polite. Do your best. Understand?'

Puso nodded.

'Good advice,' said Mr Molofololo. 'But now, Mma Ramotswe, I want to bring Rops in on this. He's the captain, you see.'

'I knew that,' said Mma Ramotswe. She smiled at Rops. 'Everybody knows about you, Rra.'

The captain inclined his head graciously. 'And everybody knows about you, Mma Ramotswe.'

She glanced at Mr Molofololo. If everybody knew about her, then it was going to be difficult for her to work on this case discreetly. And certainly there would be no possibility of her pretending to be what she was not, as Mr Molofololo had suggested earlier. 'Do they, Rra? What do they know about me?'

The captain stood up and flexed his arms. Then he put one foot in front of the other and rocked gently, stretching the muscles of his legs. 'They know that you are the private detective lady who has that place on the Tlokweng Road. Near the garage. They know about that.'

'Do they, Rra?' asked Mma Ramotswe. 'Do you think that everybody knows that? Everybody?'

Rops stopped his exercise. 'No, I am exaggerating, Mma. I happen to know that because I remember everything I read in the newspaper. But I do not think that there will be all that many people who will remember that sort of thing.'

Mr Molofololo, who had been following the exchange with interest, now interrupted. 'Would the players know, do you think, Rops?'

Rops looked thoughtful. 'No, probably not. The boys do not read the front part of the newspaper. They read the sports news and by the time they have finished reading about football their eyes are too tired to read the other pages.'

Mr Molofololo laughed. 'They are football players, you see, Mma Ramotswe. And the heads of football players are usually just full of football. They do not have any space for other thoughts.' He paused, looking appreciatively at Rops. 'Except for Rops, of course. Rops is not like that.'

Rops looked pleased with the compliment, and he gave a mock bow in the direction of Mr Molofololo. 'I do my best,' he said.

'And it is very good,' said Mr Molofololo quickly. He gestured for Rops to sit down again and then he indicated to an aide that he should take Puso out of the room. 'Take the boy to the dressing room,' he said. 'He can watch the players getting ready.'

Puso, star-struck silent but beaming with pleasure, was led away while Mma Ramotswe and the two men settled themselves around a table.

'Now, Rops,' Mr Molofololo began, 'I have told Mma Ramotswe about our problems. What I haven't told her is that you and I have talked and talked and talked and we have never got anywhere nearer a solution than when we started out. That's true, isn't it?'

Rops nodded his agreement. 'We have, Boss. I agree with you in one thing. We have not been doing as well as we should. But I do not agree with you when you say that we have a traitor in the team. Who is this man? Can you point him out to me?'

85

This seemed to irritate Mr Molofololo, who sat forward in his seat and began to drum his fingers on the table. 'I am the one. It is me. Me. If I could point him out to you, then we would not be where we are today. We would have dealt with him. And I wouldn't have had to go to a detective agency to get help. No, I cannot point to the traitor because I do not know who he is. But that does not mean that he is not there.'

For a moment nobody spoke. Rops frowned, as if he was trying to disentangle Mr Molofololo's message; Mma Ramotswe was silent because she was wondering about the significance of the words *I am the one. It is me.* It was as if he had suddenly decided to confess to being the traitor himself, which did not make sense. So what did *I am the one* mean, then?

Mma Ramotswe broke the silence. 'Excuse me, Rra,' she said. 'You said *I am the one.* What did you mean, Rra?'

Mr Molofololo looked at her as if she had raised an irrelevance. 'What did you say I said, Mma?'

'You said *I am the one.*'

He looked at Rops, who shrugged. Then he turned back to Mma Ramotswe. 'I don't think I did, Mma. We were talking about finding this man who is letting the team down. We are looking for the jackal who has crept into the herd wearing the clothes of a goat. That is what we're talking about.'

Mma Ramotswe made a gesture of acceptance. 'Very well, Rra. Let us talk about that.' She turned to face Rops. 'Rra Thobega: have you ever seen any of the players do anything that made you suspicious?'

Rops shook his head vehemently. 'Never.

Everybody plays with one-hundred-per-cent commitment. Commitment, Mma. Commitment.'

'Then why are we losing?' interjected Mr Molofololo.

'Because somebody has to lose,' said Rops.

Mma Ramotswe thought this quite a reasonable thing to say. In any game where two teams were trying to win, one would be disappointed; that was the nature of competitive games. And there were, she imagined, teams that were not very good and would therefore lose consistently.

Mr Molofololo, however, was not so impressed. 'Yes,' he said. 'Somebody has to win and somebody has to lose. But when you have a strong team like ours, then you do not expect it to be the one who will always lose, do you? We should win some games and lose others. That is the way these things work, I believe.'

Mr Molofololo stared at Rops, as if daring him to contradict such obvious logic. But the captain merely shrugged, looked at his watch, and announced that it was time for him to go to the dressing room and marshal the team.

'Then we must go and find our seats,' said Mr Molofololo, standing up and straightening his tie. 'I shall get somebody to fetch your little boy up from the dressing room, Mma, and bring him to our seats. We are all sitting together in my special place. You will have a good view from there.'

*   *   *

The game began. For Mma Ramotswe the first few minutes were reasonably interesting, as Mr Molofololo gave her a running commentary on

87

who was who and how many goals they had scored—or failed to score—over the last season. He knew each of the players intimately, she thought; in fact, it rather reminded her of the way her late father, Obed Ramotswe, had known the cattle that made up his herd. He had known the strengths of each beast—its potential to grow, its lineage, its ability to withstand drought, and so on. Mr Molofololo was like that with his players, and she expected at any moment that he would launch into a discussion of how to breed football players, but he did not; that would perhaps be taking it a bit too far.

For the first fifteen minutes or so, it seemed to her that nothing much was happening. The Kalahari Swoopers got possession of the ball and lost it from time to time to the Township Rollers. Then they got it again and the action switched back where it had been before they lost possession. Then everything changed again.

'How are we doing?' she asked Mr Molofololo at one point. And he replied, 'Nothing is happening yet, Mma. You must be patient. This is not like cooking.'

She wondered whether to take objection to that remark, but decided not to. It was not just that Mr Molofololo was the client, and one should not offend clients; there was something strange about Mr Molofololo, something that she could not quite put her finger on. He had a tendency to make remarks that were just a little bit disconcerting—as if he was thinking about something quite different, or as if he saw a dimension to an issue that you did not.

Mma Ramotswe settled into her seat and

watched the match unfold. From time to time Mr Molofololo became animated and shouted out encouragement; at other times he groaned and sank his head in his hands. And others in the audience were behaving in a similar way as the fortunes of the match flowed this way and that. It was all new to Mma Ramotswe, and she reflected on how strange it was that things like this—football matches, with all their passion and complexity—had been taking place right under her nose in Gaborone and she had known so little about them.

Puso seemed to follow exactly what was happening. He was sitting next to Mr Molofololo, and the great man occasionally leant over and discussed a point of tactics with him. At half-time, when the players went off the field and the Botswana Defence Force band marched out on to the field to play, Mma Ramotswe asked Puso how the match was going.

'Not very well,' Puso said. 'The Swoopers are going to lose, I think. Unless Quickie Chitamba can do something.'

'Quickie Chitamba? Who is this Quickie Chitamba?'

Puso looked at Mma Ramotswe with the condescending tolerance of one explaining something to another who cannot possibly understand. This was men's business, he seemed to be saying. 'Quickie Chitamba is a striker, Mma. It is his job to score goals.'

Mma Ramotswe nodded. She understood that goals were the object of the whole exercise, but could not any player score a goal?

'And the goalkeeper has to stop that, doesn't he?' she asked.

'Of course,' Puso replied. 'And we have a very good goalkeeper, Mma.'

'We?'

Puso explained again. 'Our team. Swoopers. The goalie is Big Man Tafa. He is a very good goalie.'

Mma Ramotswe nodded. 'I see. Being a big man must be a good thing if you are a goalkeeper. Big Man Tafa must block the mouth of the goal.'

Puso shook his head. 'Except he is very small, Mma.'

'Big Man Tafa is small?'

'Yes,' said Puso. 'He is very small, Mma. But he is also a very good goalkeeper.'

Mma Ramotswe was silent. She was learning a great deal about football in a very short time. She was learning about possession of the ball, about strikers and their doings, about big men who were really small; and there would be more to learn no doubt during the second half.

They returned to their seats, the band marched off, and the match began once more. Mma Ramotswe noticed that the teams were now playing in different directions and that the pace of play seemed to have increased. The crowd, that seemed to have swelled for the second half, was even more vocal, and shouts in both English and Setswana were directed forcefully towards players who were thought not to be playing too well. And then, quite unexpectedly, a goal was scored and half the stadium erupted in a roar of triumph.

Mma Ramotswe was not sure exactly what happened, but there was no doubt amongst the Swooper supporters that the goal was Big Man Tafa's fault. And Mr Molofololo, who had been watching the second half in silence, now turned to Mma Ramotswe and said, 'See, Mma? We are going to lose now. Again. We're going to lose again.'

'But there is still time for us to score a goal,' said Mma Ramotswe soothingly.

'There is only ten minutes,' said Mr Molofololo. 'We are finished, Mma. Finished.'

He spoke in such dejected tones that Mma Ramotswe's heart went out to him. He was like a little boy, she thought; this great man was like a little boy who had been beaten in some juvenile game of stones. She almost said to him, *It's just a game, you know*, but something stopped her. It was true that it was just a game, but for these people caught up in it, it seemed to be much more than that. It was more like a battle for life or death.

Defeat by one goal would have been bad enough, but there was more to come. With only a couple of minutes to go, the Township Rollers pressed home an advantage and broke through the Swoopers' defences. There was a flurry of activity and shouts from the crowd. Then another ball sailed past Big Man Tafa and the Township Rollers' supporters became ecstatic. Mr Molofololo made a gesture of disgust and turned away.

'So is Big Man the traitor?' asked Mma Ramotswe gently.

Mr Molofololo looked at her in surprise. 'Big Man? Certainly not. He has allowed a couple of goals to get past him, but you can't save everything. This isn't like cooking, Mma.'

Again the reference to cooking, and again Mma Ramotswe bit her tongue. She had had enough of

91

football, she thought, and it occurred to her that she should politely inform Mr Molofololo that she would not be able to take on the case. But if she did that, then there would be no fee, and with prices rising as they were, the No. 1 Ladies' Detective Agency could not afford to be choosy about which cases it took on and which it did not. Tlokweng Road Speedy Motors provided a reasonable income for the family, but children were expensive, whether they were one's own or whether they were foster-children like Puso and Motholeli. At the end of each month there was never very much money left over, although Mma Ramotswe was aware of how fortunate she was when compared with others. She thought of Fanwell, who gave every pula of his modest apprentice's salary to his grandmother. Compared with him, her position was comfortable indeed.

And there was another reason why she felt that she should resist the temptation to resign from the case. Mma Ramotswe had always appreciated a challenge, and although she had not been a private detective for all that long, she had never once turned down a case because she felt that it was too complicated. The world of football might be an alien one, but she had entered all sorts of unfamiliar surroundings in the course of her career and had been undaunted by them. She would have to learn a little bit more about football—she accepted that—but it appeared that she had a perfect domestic tutor on hand for that: Puso. He knew all about strikers and the like, and she would learn from him. No, she would remain on the case; there would be no resignation.

Mr Molofololo went down to the dressing room

after the match and took Puso with him, while Mma Ramotswe waited in the car. The crowd was now leaving the Stadium and she caught snippets of conversation as people walked past. *Why was Big Man on the wrong side of the goal? Did you see that?* To which the reply, cut tantalisingly short, was *Yes, you know what I think* . . . What do you think? Mma Ramotswe asked herself. She would have loved to run past the two fans and ask them: Do you think he did not save those goals deliberately? Whose side do you think he was really on?

After about ten minutes, Puso reappeared with Mr Molofololo. The owner of the Kalahari Swoopers looked extremely downcast, and his conversation on the way to drop them off at Zebra Drive was virtually monosyllabic.

'Bad,' he said. 'Very bad.'

'I'm sorry, Rra,' said Mma Ramotswe. 'I was very much hoping that you would win. But maybe the Township Rollers are just playing very strongly these days. Maybe they deserved to win.'

'No.'

'Oh well, perhaps things will be better at the next game. You never know.'

'Won't,' snapped Mr Molofololo.

After that, Mma Ramotswe was silent. Then, as the driver brought the large car to a halt outside the house on Zebra Drive, she spoke to Mr Molofololo again. She reminded him that when he had first come to see her they had spoken of her being given a list of all the names of the players, along with their addresses. Could Mr Molofololo provide that?

'Yes.'

Mma Ramotswe opened the car door. 'We have

had a very good afternoon, Rra. Thank you very much for that. And Puso . . .'

Puso took his cue and thanked Mr Molofololo for allowing him to watch the game. This produced a rather better response, and an offer to take the boy to the match that the Swoopers would play the following weekend. Would he like that?

The boy looked pleadingly at Mma Ramotswe, who nodded. 'I would like that very much, Rra,' he said. 'Thank you.'

They got out of the car and went into the house.

'I am so happy, Mma,' said Puso.

Mma Ramotswe patted him affectionately on the head. 'I can tell that. And I am glad that you are happy, Puso, even if it seems that the Swoopers themselves are not very happy.'

'Oh, I think they are happy,' said Puso. 'I do not think they wanted to win very much.'

Mma Ramotswe frowned. The little boy was about to go off to his bedroom but she reached out to grab his arm. 'Puso! Why did you say that?'

The boy shrugged his shoulders. 'Oh, I could tell,' he said. 'One of them even smiled when the Township Rollers scored that first goal. I saw him.'

Mma Ramotswe's eyes widened. 'He smiled? One of the players?'

'Yes. I was watching him, and I saw him smile. Then he suddenly stopped smiling, as if somebody had told him he mustn't.'

Mma Ramotswe stared at Puso. What was that expression that somebody had used the other day, and she had noted down as a very useful thing to say? *Out of the mouths of babes* . . . Yes, that was it.

She tried not to sound too concerned. You had to be careful when getting information from

94

children; you had to be careful that you did not encourage them to embroider things. Clovis Andersen, author of *The Principles of Private Detection*, had written about that, she remembered. *Always be very cautious when getting evidence from children*, he advised. *Never let the child think that you want a particular answer, because if you do that, the child will make something up in order to oblige. I have been involved in many cases where apparently valuable information from children has proved to be misleading because the child was trying to be helpful. Children, in general, do not have a clear idea of the distinction between what the world is and what we want it to be.*

Clovis Andersen was right about that, as he was about so much, and Mma Ramotswe suspected that Mma Potokwani, with all her experience of children, would concur. One of the children at the orphan farm had happened to witness a burglary in a neighbouring house and Mma Potokwani had sat with the child while he made the statement to the police. The boy, who was barely seven, had said that the man he saw breaking in through the window was Santa Claus. The police had tried to shift him from this, but he was adamant. 'It was Santa Claus,' he had said.

So now, affecting nonchalance, Mma Ramotswe sought to elicit information about the player who had smiled when the opposition had scored a goal. 'Oh, I expect he was smiling about something else,' she said. 'Perhaps he was remembering a joke, or something like that. I don't think it's very important, anyway.'

'I don't think he was thinking of a joke,' said Puso solemnly. 'He was smiling because the

95

Township Rollers had scored a goal. I'm sure he was, Mma.'

Mma Ramotswe shrugged, as if to suggest that the matter was not very important. 'Who was he, by the way? Did you see which player it was?'

Puso scratched his head. 'I think it was Quickie Chitamba,' he said. 'Or maybe it wasn't. Maybe it was another man who looked like Quickie.' He paused. 'No, I don't think it was Quickie.'

'Oh well,' said Mma Ramotswe.

CHAPTER EIGHT

VIOLET SEPHOTHO STARTS WORK

On the Monday following the Kalahari Swoopers' ignominious defeat by the Township Rollers, a new employee presented herself for work at Mr Phuti Radiphuti's Double Comfort Furniture Shop. This was none other than Violet Sephotho, formerly an undistinguished student at the Botswana Secretarial College, where she definitely did *not* get the eighty per cent that she had claimed at interview. It was the same Violet Sephotho whom Mma Makutsi had met again at the Botswana Academy of Dance and Movement, the Tuesday evening dance class at the President Hotel, where Violet, determined to belittle someone who had done so much better in the college exams, had shown herself at her most disparaging and condescending.

It was also the same Violet Sephotho with whom Mma Makutsi had subsequently crossed swords on two occasions. The first of these had been when Mma Makutsi had rather too hastily tendered her resignation to Mma Ramotswe and had gone to an employment agency to find another job, only to discover that the agency was run by Violet. This, of course, gave Violet the opportunity to make snide and cutting remarks about the harshness of the current employment climate to women who were not very prepossessing in their appearance—by which she meant Mma Makutsi herself—and to suggest that perhaps she should look for a job outside Gaborone, in a place like Lobatse, possibly, where standards were not so high. An unfashionable-looking person, she suggested, could find a job in Lobatse even if she could not do so in Gaborone.

Mma Makutsi had stormed out of that interview and had tried to forget about Violet Sephotho. In this she had succeeded until Violet had cropped up again as the writer, both she and Mma Ramotswe had suspected, of a series of anonymous letters of an insulting nature, some of which made reference to large glasses. That had resulted in a spectacular chase through the aisles of the supermarket at the River Walk shopping centre, and since then Violet had not been heard of nor seen. And now here she was, turning up in the very heart of Mma Makutsi's camp, as a new employee—in the beds section—of the Double Comfort Furniture Shop.

Phuti was unaware of the full perfidy of his new employee. He had detected a certain coldness on his fiancée's part when he had mentioned that he had given Violet a job, but he had put this down to some old rivalry at the Botswana Secretarial College—a minor clash of personalities, perhaps—

that would soon be forgotten. He had no idea, of course, that Violet had come to work in his shop with a very clear aim. Mma Makutsi, being a woman, had worked out what this aim was, whereas a man, particularly a trusting and rather innocent man like Phuti, would never suspect.

'So, Mma,' he said when Violet reported to the office early on Monday morning. 'You are here in good time. It is only . . .' He looked at his watch. The shop opened at eight o'clock and it was barely half past seven.

Violet smiled at him. 'I always like to be at work on time,' she said. 'It is best to be completely ready when the first customers come. I have always thought that, Rra.'

Phuti nodded his approval. 'That is the best attitude,' he said. 'I have seen customers walk out of shops because the staff were not ready to assist them.'

'I cannot stand that sort of thing,' said Violet. 'The customer is always right.'

Again Phuti indicated his approval. 'That is rule number one in this establishment,' he said. 'And I'm very glad that you know that, Mma.'

'Please call me Violet, Rra,' she said. 'I would prefer that. It is more friendly, I think.'

'If you wish, Mma. I usually call members of my staff by their first names, if that is what they want.'

'I do want it, Rra. You can even call me Vi, if you wish. Some people who are very close to me call me that. It is short for Violet, you see.'

After Violet had signed the staff contract Phuti accompanied her to the new beds section, where she was to preside as assistant manager. Then he began to show her the beds and to tell her about

98

the relative merits of each of the ten or so models that they carried.

'Most of the beds we stock are double beds,' he said.

'That is nice,' said Violet. 'That is less lonely. Who wants a single bed these days?'

Phuti frowned. 'There is some demand,' he said. 'Sometimes a person whose spouse is late, for example, might ask for a single bed. Or there are grandmothers. They like single beds if their husband is a bad snorer.'

Violet giggled. 'I never snore,' she said.

Phuti said nothing. 'And these beds over here,' he went on to explain. 'They are the most expensive beds we have. They are what we call de luxe, first-class beds. They have very comfortable mattresses. Very soft. Very springy.'

'Very nice beds for a newly married couple,' said Violet. She lowered her eyes slightly as she spoke, in a manner suggestive of modesty, indeed suggestive in every sense. But Phuti saw only the modesty, and was impressed. He had wondered whether Violet was a bit forward, but this demure remark pointed to a nature quite in keeping with the ethos of the bed department of the Double Comfort Furniture Shop.

He showed her the desk where she would sit, and the filing system for customer systems.

'I am very familiar with filing systems,' Violet said. 'I studied them a lot at the Botswana Secretarial College—all different types of filing systems: alphabetical, numerical . . . and other types. All of them.'

Phuti smiled. 'Ah, the Botswana Secretarial College! Of course, you knew my fiancée there—

99

you told me that. Grace.'

'Makutsi,' said Violet quickly, breaking into a smile. 'Grace Makutsi. Of course, I knew her. We all knew her. She was very popular with everybody.'

'That is good to hear,' said Phuti. 'It would not do to marry an unpopular lady, would it?'

Phuti was not particularly good at witty remarks and this was about as witty as he became. But Violet showed her appreciation by bursting out laughing, which pleased him, as she suspected it would.

'Yes,' she said. 'She was very popular with all the girls . . . and the boys too. Very popular with the boys.'

Phuti gave a start. He smiled, but the smile was a nervous one. 'The boys too? But there were no boys, surely, at the Botswana Secretarial College, were there?'

Violet sat down at her desk and toyed with a ball-point pen. She did not look at Phuti as she spoke, but stared somewhere behind and beyond him, as if casting her mind back to the events of a distant, barely remembered past. 'No, there were no boys at the college itself. But there were always boys at the gate, if you know what I mean.'

She glanced at Phuti before her gaze slid away again, off to that distant point. 'There was a café near the gate, you see, and this was very popular. All the boys knew that at the end of classes the girls from the college would go to this café and sit around. So the boys always went there so that they could sit around with the girls and chat to them. We used to call it the dating shop. Hah! The dating shop. Those were the days, Rra.'

For a few moments Phuti said nothing. Then he cleared his throat and began to speak. His stutter, which now only came at moments of stress, emerged, but only slightly, like the top of a treacherous rock lurking under the surface of a river. 'Di . . . di . . . did Grace go to this ca . . . café?'

'Oh yes,' said Violet. 'Grace was the life and soul of the café. A big magnet for the boys. Wow! You should have seen her.'

Phuti tried to laugh, but even the laugh had a strangled sound to it. Violet watched him, and her pleasure showed. 'Yes, those were certainly the days. But you know something? Even today, a few years on, I look back on those times and think: the years may come and go, but none of us really changes, do we? I'm still the same person I was in those days . . .' And here she paused, before continuing, 'And you must be the same person you were then. And Grace, too. She won't have changed, I think.'

Phuti said nothing. There was something desperate about his manner, and he began to tug at the right cuff of his shirt with his left hand. Violet's arrows had gone home, and she knew it. It was time, though, to change the direction of her campaign. It was always possible to get a man away from a woman and one had to be careful not to overplay one's hand at the beginning. But she was confident that she could do it. She had done it twice before, although on those occasions the men in question had been mere temporary entertainment and had been abandoned once the novelty wore off. This was different. Phuti would not be temporary entertainment—in fact, he could not be considered entertainment in any sense of the word. But a woman reached a stage in life where her goals changed, and the most important of these was undoubtedly the security of landing a comfortably-off husband.

Phuti was ideal: a mild, unobtrusive man who could be twisted round one's little finger. Perfect. And the fact that he was engaged to be married to Grace Makutsi, assistant detective at the No. 1 Ladies' Detective Agency and distinguished graduate of the Botswana Secretarial College (ninety-seven per cent)? Pah! Not an obstacle at all; a tiny anthill at the most, to be kicked aside by the effortless stride of a fashionable pair of shoes as they went by.

*   *   *

Mma Makutsi, of course, knew nothing of this conversation between Phuti Radiphuti and Violet Sephotho. At the time that it took place, though, she was none the less thinking of Violet and of the threat that this dangerous, ruthless woman presented. Phuti had told her that Monday morning was to be his new employee's first day in the Double Comfort Furniture Shop and ever since she had woken up that morning she had been unable to get the thought of Violet out of her mind.

As she travelled in to work on the crowded minibus, she noticed a heavily-made-up woman in the seat in front of her. The woman had applied such a thick layer of cream to her skin that when the morning sun slanted in through the minibus window, it flashed off her face, as if off a signalling mirror. Miles away, thought Mma Makutsi, miles away up in the hills overlooking the dam, they might spot this flash of light and wonder what message was being sent to whom. No, that was a ridiculous thought, but look at her, Mma Makutsi said to herself, she's every bit as bad as . . . Violet Sephotho came to mind again, no matter how hard she tried to think about other things. And when the woman in the front turned and smiled at somebody at her side, Mma Makutsi found herself thinking: *flirt*, just like Violet Sephotho; unable to keep her eyes, and her hands, no doubt, off men. Such women were a danger to the public and the Government should put up large warning signs like those health notices you saw. These would say: *Watch Out for Women Like This!* And underneath would be a picture of Violet Sephotho, or somebody looking quite like her.

In normal circumstances, thoughts like these might have helped; an amusing fantasy about a troublesome opponent may defuse the threat that the opponent presents; in normal circumstances . . . but these were not normal times at all; far from it. These were times of war, even if hostilities had not yet been formally declared. And this realisation induced a sinking feeling in Mma Makutsi because she realised that Violet Sephotho had a weapon in her armoury that she simply did not have. Glamour.

That was the worst of it—that dreadful conclusion. I am a lady with glasses, thought Mma Makutsi. I need the glasses to see. I am also a lady with a certain skin problem. That is not my fault, and there is not all that much you can do about your skin. We are given a skin at the beginning, and that is our skin. If the skin you have has some blotches, then you have to find a man who does not mind about these things—a man who looks at you, sees your skin, and then goes under the skin to see what lies beneath; to see whether the person inside the skin can cook, or likes to listen to him, or can keep a house and a yard neat and clean, and will be kind to his aged father—even if the aged father makes strange noises when he is eating, and often even when he is not eating. That is what you *hope* a man will look for under a blotchy skin.

But unfortunately men are weak. They may know that they should look for these finer qualities in a woman, but they do not always do it. They see, instead, the clothes that a woman wears, and they look at her figure and the way she walks, and at the bright things she puts in her hair—beads, silver combs and the like—and they cannot help it, poor men, they are dazzled, just as a mouse is hypnotised by the swaying of a cobra. And then the cobra strikes and it is all over for the mouse, just as it is for the man. For the mouse, it ends in a quick scuffle of dust and a few convulsive movements; for the man, it ends in the noise and fuss of a wedding, when all the uncles and aunts, especially the aunts, come up to him and surround him and touch and prod him and then he is finished and that is the end of the man.

Mma Makutsi looked out of the minibus window. Violet Sephotho. Violet Sephotho. Very well, Violet Sephotho: I am a peaceful woman, and I do not like to be at daggers drawn with anybody. But there comes a time when you have to defend what you have. Phuti Radiphuti is mine and I will fight to the end to keep him. To the very end.

The minibus was now on the Tlokweng Road, approaching the stop at which Mma Makutsi would alight. She felt much better after that stirring piece of self-addressed rhetoric, and as she stepped down from the minibus she caught sight of the small doughnut tuck-stand that she frequented on a Friday, as a treat. Today was only a Monday but she would indulge herself, she thought. She would buy a doughnut for herself—a rich, greasy, sugar-dusted doughnut—and one for Mma Ramotswe too. They would eat them together over their morning tea, in companionable enjoyment—two ladies sharing a common office, but two friends as well, united as friends so often are, in the love of the things they loved.

CHAPTER NINE

THE TINY WHITE VAN IN PERIL

'That was very good, Mma Makutsi,' said Mma Ramotswe, licking the sugar off the tips of her fingers. 'There is a lot to be said for starting the week with a doughnut.' She picked the last few crumbs off her plate and popped them into her mouth. 'Up to now, we have been finishing the week with a doughnut. Maybe we should change and start the week with one.'

'Or we could start *and* finish the week with one,' said Mma Makutsi. 'That would always be possible.'

Mma Ramotswe struggled with temptation for a moment, but only for a moment. 'That would be a very good policy, Mma.' And not only did it strike her as being very attractive from the point of view of personal satisfaction, but it also made sense in terms of staff morale. She had read a magazine article recently in which the author, described as a *famous expert*, had written that any employer wishing to get the best out of staff should introduce a system of staff perks. *Small privileges are always welcome*, he wrote. *A staff outing not only provides pleasure, it bonds staff together and motivates them*. Mma Ramotswe thought that staff outings were undoubtedly a good idea, but she did not feel that they were necessarily a good thing for a business as small as hers. She and Mma Makutsi had plenty of opportunities to bond when they sat in their little office together; indeed, they had been bonding from the day that Mma Makutsi had first arrived and talked herself into a job. And if they were to go on an outing together, where would they go? It was all very well for people who worked in places like Johannesburg to talk about going on staff outings; there were plenty of places to go to in a city of that size. Gaborone was so much smaller and there were few places that she and Mma Makutsi could go to that they would not have already been to many times before.

They could go and have tea in the café on River Walk, the one where you could sit and look out over the car park with the eucalyptus trees in the distance, but they could just as easily have tea in the office and, with minimum craning of the neck, see the edge of that very same stand of eucalyptus trees. Or they could go down to Mokolodi and have tea in the restaurant there; that was perhaps a bit more exciting, but it would require a half-hour trip in the tiny white van to get there and the tiny white van was not really in a position to make such a trip at present. It was true that it was running, but only just; walking, perhaps, would have been a better word to describe it.

She pushed her plate to the side of her desk. The thought of her van filled her with dread. That morning Mr J. L. B. Matekoni had left for work first, and when Mma Ramotswe arrived he was standing in front of the garage, chatting to Fanwell when the tiny white van limped into its parking place at the side of the building. Seeing him, Mma Ramotswe had put her foot down on the accelerator, hoping that the van might just rise to the occasion and drive up at a normal speed. It had not, and the sudden strain on the engine had produced a frightening grinding sound, more serious, it seemed, than any noise the van had previously emitted.

Mr J. L. B. Matekoni broke off his conversation with his apprentice and walked briskly over to the van.

'What a terrible sound,' he said. 'Mma Ramotswe! How long has your van been making that sound?'

Mma Ramotswe swallowed hard. 'A sound, Mr J. L. B. Matekoni? You say that it's making a strange sound? Are you sure it was not some other vehicle?' She looked desperately over her shoulder to see if anything was passing on the Tlokweng Road. The road was quite empty.

'No, it is your van,' he said. 'There must be something very wrong with it. I'll take a look at it right away. We've got a couple of hours before the next job is due in.'

Mma Ramotswe realised that she had no escape. 'I don't want to be any trouble,' she muttered. 'Maybe some other time.'

'Nonsense!' said Mr J. L. B. Matekoni. 'I am your husband, Mma. I cannot have my own wife driving round in a van that makes a noise like that. Think of my reputation—just think of it. What would they say?' He looked at her reproachfully before answering his own question. 'They would say that I was not much of a mechanic if that was the sound that my own wife's van made. Everyone would be saying that.'

Mma Ramotswe caught Fanwell's eye. He shrugged, as if to say, *I told you, Mma Ramotswe. I told you that there was no hope.*

She went into the office, her heart quite cold within her. She knew what would happen, and that a mechanical sentence of doom, uttered in words as powerful and as grave as those of any doctor imparting bad news, would soon be uttered. She decided, though, that there was no point in doing anything but put it out of her mind for the time being. When there is nothing you can do to stop the march of adverse events, then the best thing, she felt, was to get on with life and not to worry. And at that particular moment, Mma Makutsi had come in with the doughnuts, which would be a balm, if only a temporary one, to the anxiety she felt.

And there was plenty to do. When Mma Makutsi arrived in the office that morning, she had found a large envelope tucked under the door, emanating, according to what was written on the outside, from the office of Mr Leungo Molofololo.

'I've been expecting that,' said Mma Ramotswe,

examining the neatly typed sheets of paper that Mma Makutsi handed over to her. 'This is the list of the players. This is where we start, Mma.'

Mma Makutsi, standing behind Mma Ramotswe and looking over her shoulder, pointed to one of the names. 'Big Man,' she said. 'What stupid names these footballers have, Mma. They are just boys. Small boys.'

Mma Ramotswe smiled indulgently. She would not have put it quite like that, but she knew what Mma Makutsi meant. Women did not give one another nicknames. For some reason it was always men, and the names chosen were indeed absurd: private jokes that meant nothing to others; a small humiliation hung around the neck of some unfortunate. Why, she wondered, did men behave like this? You would think that they would learn— and some of them were learning, a bit—but most of them did not. 'I know all about Big Man,' she said. 'He's the goalkeeper and he is very small. He's not big at all.'

'There you are,' said Mma Makutsi. 'That proves it. Why call a small man Big Man? That is very stupid—just as I said.' She peered at the list. 'And who is this man called Rops? It says here that he is the captain. Why is he called Rops?'

'Rops is a name I have heard before,' said Mma Ramotswe. 'It is a perfectly good name. Unlike this one here. You see that he is called Joel "Two Feet" Koko.'

'Another silly name,' said Mma Makutsi. She moved back to her desk and sat expectantly. 'Well now, Mma Ramotswe, what do we do with this list? How do we find the traitor?'

Mma Ramotswe laid the list down. 'Let's think,

Mma Makutsi. What have we done in the past?'

Mma Makutsi looked puzzled. 'We've never had anything to do with a football team, Mma. Not that I recall.'

'I know that,' said Mma Ramotswe. 'But we have had to deal with dishonest employees, haven't we? And the simplest way of finding people like that is to see who's richer than he should be. That's always a good way of exposing somebody who's being paid to do something dishonest or who has his fingers in the till.'

Mma Makutsi contemplated this. It was, she agreed, the best first step, but would it necessarily work in this case? What if the traitor acted for some reason other than a financial one? People betrayed others, their country even, for so many different reasons: because they had a score to settle with their employer, because they were in love with somebody who wanted them to commit the act of betrayal, because of jealousy; there were as many sorts of reasons as there were sorts of people.

Mma Ramotswe saw the logic in this. 'Yes,' she agreed. 'It is always possible that there is somebody in the team who is feeling angry with Mr Molofololo. Perhaps there is somebody who thinks he should be captain instead of Rops. If you were that person, and you thought that you should be playing up in the front, where all the opportunities to score goals will be had, then you might think, *I'll show him*. You might think that, might you not, Mma Makutsi?'

Mma Makutsi confirmed that she might. So Mma Ramotswe continued, 'And what if you were a footballer who had a girlfriend and this girlfriend was stolen away by the owner of the team or even the captain? What then? You might also say, *I'll show them.*'

Mma Makutsi listened to this intently. The stealing of a girlfriend was not all that different from the stealing of a fiancé. And that made her mouth go dry with fear. What if Violet succeeded in stealing Phuti, as she so clearly planned to do? What future would there be then for her, for Grace Makutsi? She would never find another man, she feared, or at least she would never find one half as nice as Phuti, let alone one who had his own shop and a great number of cattle. She would continue to be an assistant detective all her days, a woman who had to watch her pennies and see other women, married women, leading more comfortable lives because they had men to go out and earn a living for them. Oh, the injustice of it; oh, the hateful, hateful thought.

She became aware that Mma Ramotswe had said something. 'What was that, Mma? I was thinking of something else.'

'I pointed out that we already have a bit of help here from Mr Molofololo,' said Mma Ramotswe. 'You may have noticed that there is a tick against three names on the list. That is something that I asked him to do. And do you know what that means, Mma? Can you guess?'

Mma Makutsi could only guess that these were the ones whom Mr Molofololo himself suspected. But no, said Mma Ramotswe, that would be too simple. 'Remember what Clovis Andersen says, Mma,' she warned. 'He said that you should never take account of those who may be suspected by others because that may lead you up the wrong track altogether. That is what he said, Mma. And I think he is right. So these are not Mr Molofololo's suspects—it is something much simpler. The names ticked are those members of the team *who drive a Mercedes-Benz.*'

Mma Makutsi looked surprised. 'Is there something dishonest about driving a car like that, Mma?'

Mma Ramotswe laughed. 'Of course not. They are very fine cars and some very honest people drive them. No, there is another reason. A Mercedes-Benz is not a cheap car. So if somebody drives one, then there must at least have been some money. So, if you are looking for signs of money, follow the Mercedes-Benz, Mma!'

Their conversation was interrupted at this intriguing point by the entry into the office of Mr Polopetsi, the half-trained mechanic employed by Mr J. L. B. Matekoni in the garage, who occasionally helped out in the detective agency. Mr Polopetsi had been taken on as an act of charity but had proved himself to be a valuable member of staff, now quite capable of carrying out a full service on most makes of car and every bit as accomplished as the apprentices in handling a number of other mechanical procedures. He came in now bearing the chipped white mug from which he drank his tea.

'I see that you have had doughnuts,' he said, looking pointedly at the greasy wrapping paper on the side of Mma Makutsi's desk. 'I thought doughnuts were for Friday.'

'There has been a change of policy,' said Mma Makutsi. 'A forward-looking business must be flexible.'

Mma Ramotswe laughed. She was looking at Mr Polopetsi and she remembered that he was often rather good at shedding light on a problem. His ideas were frequently unusual but quite astute for all their unexpectedness.

'Tell me, Mr Polopetsi,' she asked. 'How would you deal with this thing, Rra?' She passed him Mr Molofololo's list of football players. 'Do you recognise that?'

Mr Polopetsi ran an eye down the list of names and then looked up with a grin. 'The Kalahari Swoopers, Mma. That's who these people are.' He pointed to one of the names. 'Quickie Chitamba. He used to live out at Tlokweng, near my cousin. They saw him sometimes, driving past the house. His wife is a friend of my wife's brother.'

Mma Ramotswe gave a casual wave of the hand. 'Yes,' she said. 'Quickie Chitamba. I've seen him play.'

Mr Polopetsi looked at her in astonishment. 'I would never have guessed, Mma. You're interested in football, Mma Ramotswe? I didn't know that!'

'There are always new things to find out about a person,' said Mma Makutsi.

'Oh, I know that,' said Mr Polopetsi. 'It's just that I can't see Mma Ramotswe at a football match.' He closed his eyes, the better to envisage the scene. 'No, Mma, I can't see you there. I just can't.'

Mma Ramotswe laughed. 'And that is not surprising, Rra. I have only been once. You see, we're working on a football case now. You may smile, Rra, but that is what we're doing. We are football detectives now.'

While Mma Makutsi made Mr Polopetsi a cup

113

of tea, Mma Ramotswe explained the background to the Molofololo case. Mr Polopetsi listened intently, raising an eyebrow at the allegation of treachery. When she had finished, he shook his head in wonderment. 'I noticed that they were not doing very well. I thought that maybe their coach was trying new tactics, or something like that. I would never have dreamed that there was somebody deliberately losing. That is very serious, Mma. Ow!'

'So, Mr Polopetsi,' Mma Ramotswe said. 'So here are Mma Makutsi and I sitting and wondering where to start. And I said to Mma Makutsi that we should look at anybody in the team who appears to have more money than one might expect. That's always a clue, I think.'

Mr Polopetsi scratched his head. 'Well, maybe. Maybe.'

'You don't sound convinced.'

'I said maybe, Mma. I didn't say no. I said maybe.'

Mma Ramotswe pointed to the list. 'You see, what we have done is to get Mr Molofololo to mark who has a Mercedes-Benz. We can start with those ones.'

For a few moments Mr Polopetsi looked at Mma Ramotswe doubtfully. Then he shook his head. 'Because those people will be the ones who have money they're not entitled to? Bribes? Is that what you're saying, Mma?'

Mma Ramotswe sat back in her chair. 'More or less, Rra.'

Mma Makutsi passed him his mug of tea and he nursed it carefully before raising it to his lips. 'Thank you, Mma. This is very good tea.' He took

114

a sip and then lowered the mug. 'Absolutely not, Mma Ramotswe,' he said firmly. 'You can forget about those ones.'

'Why?'

'Because football players are no fools,' said Mr Polopetsi. 'They know that they are in the public eye. They are watched all the time. People write about them in the papers. People talk. If you had money you were not entitled to, then a Mercedes-Benz is the last thing you would buy.'

Mma Makutsi leaned forward over her desk. 'He may be right, Mma Ramotswe. I can see what he means. Don't buy a Mercedes-Benz if you don't want people to start asking questions.'

Mma Ramotswe had not expected such a firm rejection of her theory, which, after all, had the stamp of Clovis Andersen's authority to it. But now that she thought of what Mr Polopetsi had said, she realised that he was probably right. It was a pity, as she thought that the Mercedes-Benz theory had its strong points, not the least of which was that it gave them a convenient starting point. But on mature reflection she decided that Mr Polopetsi was right. It would be a foolish man who invited attention where none was wanted.

And then Mr Polopetsi had an idea. It was a qualification, really, to the proposition that he had advanced earlier. 'Of course,' he said, 'their mothers are a different matter. If the mother of a football player has a Mercedes-Benz, then there is every reason to be suspicious.'

CHAPTER TEN

A BIT OF BOTSWANA'S HISTORY

Throughout the rest of that morning, Mma Ramotswe could settle to nothing. She had some letters to write and these she dictated to Mma Makutsi, whose pencil hovered over the pad while Mma Ramotswe struggled to keep her thoughts from wandering. It was the tiny white van, of course, that was preying on her mind. She felt as a relative might feel in a hospital waiting room, anticipating the results of an operation, ready to judge the outcome by the expression on the surgeon's face. In this case her vigil was made all the more trying by the fact that she could hear noises coming from the garage, a clanking sound at one point, a thudding of metal on metal at another; at least relatives of those in hospital were not treated to quite such vivid and immediate sound effects.

'You have already said that, Mma Ramotswe,' Mma Makutsi pointed out politely. 'You have already said that you will be available for a meeting on that day. Now I think you need to say . . .'

'Oh, I cannot concentrate, Mma,' said Mma Ramotswe. 'I'm sitting here and just through the wall over there my van is being taken to pieces. And it will not be good news, you know, at the end of it all.'

Mma Makutsi thought that this was probably true, but she did her best to comfort her employer. 'You never know, Mma. There are miracles from time to time. There could be a miracle for your van.'

Mma Ramotswe appreciated this but knew that there would be no miracle. And when Mr J. L. B. Matekoni came into the office half an hour or so later, wiping his hands on a piece of lint, she knew in an instant what was to come.

'I'm very sorry, Mma Ramotswe,' he began. 'The engine is just too old . . .'

He did not finish, for Mma Ramotswe had let out a wail and Mma Makutsi had leapt to her feet to comfort her.

'Don't cry, Mma,' said Mma Makutsi. 'You mustn't cry.'

Mr J. L. B. Matekoni stood awkwardly witnessing this show of female distress and the solidarity it provoked. He would have liked to have comforted his wife, too, to put his arm about her, but he was still covered in grease and this seemed to him now to be a moment to which he could add little. So he inclined his head and slipped discreetly out of the office, leaving the two women together.

'I'm sure that he'll get you another van,' said Mma Makutsi. 'And you'll come to love that one too. You'll see.'

Mma Ramotswe struggled to control herself. 'I should not cry over a little thing like this,' she sniffed. 'There are big things to cry over, such big things, and I am wasting my tears. It is only a van.'

'It's a van you have loved a lot,' said Mma Makutsi. 'I know how it feels.' She had loved her lace handkerchief, a small thing really, but one which for a time had been her only special possession. Everything else had been entirely functional, designed to meet the requirements of a life of poverty and hardship; that handkerchief had been about beauty, and fineness, and the possibility of something better.

'It is like a bit of Botswana's history,' said Mma Ramotswe. 'It is like a bit of Botswana's history that is about to be thrown on the heap. Just like that.'

Mma Makutsi was not entirely convinced by this analogy but at least it gave her an idea. 'Perhaps the museum would take it,' she ventured. 'They have some old ox-carts there. Your van could stand beside them.'

Mma Ramotswe thought this unlikely. They would not want an old white van; there were plenty of old vehicles about and there was no reason for her van to be singled out. She was not famous in any way, and nobody would be interested in a van just because she had driven it. She pointed this out to Mma Makutsi, who shook her head vigorously. 'Museums are very interested in ordinary things these days,' she said. 'They like to show how life is for ordinary people—for you and me.'

As Mma Makutsi spoke, Mma Ramotswe imagined how the museum might have a section devoted to ordinary people themselves, perhaps keeping a few ordinary people on display, sitting in chairs or reading newspapers, cooking possibly, washing their clothes, and so on. Mma Makutsi herself could be an exhibit, or at least her glasses could be on show in a special case, together with her ninety-seven-per-cent certificate from the Botswana Secretarial College. Some people might be interested in that—Mma Makutsi, for one.

'Good,' said Mma Makutsi. 'I see you are smiling. You'll feel better soon, Mma. It's not the

118

end of the world, you know.'

*   *   *

But it was—or so it increasingly seemed to Mma Ramotswe as the day wore on. She ate her lunch alone at her desk—Mma Makutsi had shopping to do—and when Mr J. L. B. Matekoni popped his head round the door to say that he was going off on some errand, she barely heard him, hardly acknowledged him. She was not to know that his errand was to a colleague in the motor trade, whom he had telephoned that morning to arrange for the purchase of a van, a small blue one, that had done a relatively low mileage and that was described, in the language of the trade, as 'very clean'.

This van he brought back to Tlokweng Road Speedy Motors less than an hour later. He parked it outside the entrance to the garage and went inside to fetch Mma Ramotswe.

'You just come outside and see something,' he said, taking her hand.

For a moment she thought that he might be leading her to see her triumphantly restored van; but then she thought, no, that cannot be—he has bought a new one. He seemed pleased and excited, and she made an effort to smile. He may not understand how I feel about my old van, she thought, but he is trying to do his best for me and I must make him think I am pleased.

The two apprentices, who were standing conspiratorially at the entrance to the garage, watched as Mr J. L. B. Matekoni led her round the side of the building. Charlie made a thumbs-up

119

sign, a sign of encouragement. Fanwell did nothing; he caught Mma Ramotswe's eye and then looked away.

'There,' said Mr J. L. B. Matekoni. 'There it is!'

The blue van was parked under the acacia tree, in the precise spot that the old van used to occupy. It was slightly bigger than the tiny white van—a medium-sized blue van, one might say—and it had been lovingly washed and polished, its chrome fittings glinting even in the shade of the tree.

Mma Ramotswe stopped in her tracks. 'It is a very beautiful van,' she said. She made a supreme effort to sound enthusiastic, but it was hard. She swallowed. 'Very beautiful.' She turned to face her husband. 'And you have bought it for me?'

Mr J. L. B. Matekoni inclined his head graciously. 'I have bought it for you, Mma Ramotswe. It is yours. Your new van.'

She reached out to take his hand, and squeezed it. 'You are a good husband,' she whispered. 'You are a kind man.'

He looked proud. 'It is no more than you deserve.'

He led her by the hand to stand beside the new van. She saw herself reflected in its gleaming surface; a white van would reflect nothing—the world vanished beside it—but in the blue of this van there was a traditionally built woman standing beside a man in khaki. Both were distorted, as in a mischievous hall of mirrors; the man had become squat, mostly trunk, with stunted limbs; the woman had become more traditionally built than ever—a wide expanse of woman, bulging like the continent of Africa itself.

Mr J. L. B. Matekoni reached forward and

120

opened the driver's door. The old van's door had squeaked when opened; this one moved silently on well-greased hinges, revealing a pristine interior. It was hard to believe that the van was not brand new, that it had not rolled fresh from a factory floor down in Port Elizabeth.

Everything was in place, and perfect. On the floor, which was covered with a dark rubber mat, specially cut squares of paper had been laid to protect the shoes of the driver; and on this paper was printed the motto of the garage that had supplied the van: *At Your Service, Sir!* Or Madam, thought Mma Ramotswe, although she understood that cars and vans were usually the preoccupation of men, while women thought of keeping families going, of the home, of making the world a bit more beautiful and comfortable, of the stemming of humanity's tears. Or some women did. And some men, too, did not think of cars.

Mr J. L. B. Matekoni gestured that Mma Ramotswe should get in. 'It is all ready to drive,' he said. 'We can go down the road and back again. You can get the feel of it and I can help you with anything.'

Again she forced a smile. She tried to show her gratitude, for she did feel gratitude, profound gratitude, that she had a husband like this, who loved her so, he would seek out a special van for her and make a gift of it.

'It is very beautiful, Rra,' she said. 'And this blue. It is like the sky.'

'That is why I chose it,' he said. 'They had a red van, but I said no. You were not a person to drive a red vehicle. I told them that. Red vehicles are for young men.' He tossed his head in the direction of the two apprentices, who were watching from a distance. 'You know how young men are.'

She knew. But she also remembered her visit to Fanwell's house, and learning that his entire salary kept that large family alive. She could not talk about this, though. The mission had been a clandestine one, so she could not say, *Well, there are some young men who do good things*—which is what she would have said otherwise.

She lowered herself into the driver's seat. It felt so different from the seat of the old van, which was much smaller and less padded. Over the years, though, the tiny white van's seat had moulded to her particular shape, with the result that it was like a supporting hand beneath her. This seat was an alien shape; it might give in the right places in the future, but for now, comfortable though it was, it felt unfamiliar and rather disconcerting. Driving along in such a seat would be a bit like driving an armchair, Mma Ramotswe thought, but did not say. What she said to Mr J. L. B. Matekoni was, 'It is the last word in comfort, Rra. It is very, very comfortable. Surely this seat comes from the Double Comfort Furniture Shop!'

He appreciated the joke. 'Maybe, Mma Ramotswe. Maybe. We shall have to ask Phuti Radiphuti about it.'

Mr J. L. B. Matekoni walked round the front of the van and got into the passenger seat. 'We can go for a drive now,' he said. 'That is the ignition there. See? See how easily the engine starts. And listen— listen to how quiet it is.'

Mma Ramotswe had to admit that the engine was indeed quiet. But then, 'Where are the gears, Rra?'

Mr J. L. B. Matekoni laughed. 'Gears are largely a thing of the past, Mma Ramotswe. Or at least changing them is a thing of the past. This is an automatic van.'

Mma Ramotswe had been in an automatic vehicle before but had not paid much attention to what was going on. She remembered thinking that some people might find it useful not to have to change gear all the time, but she was not sure whether she was one of those drivers. In fact, she felt that she probably was not, as she found that leaving one hand on the gear lever and steering with the other was a comfortable driving position. She suspected, too, that Mma Potokwani would agree with her; the matron of the orphan farm, Mma Ramotswe had observed, changed gear in the same way as she stirred the mixture for one of her famous fruit cakes: with vigour and a strong circular movement.

Over the next fifteen minutes, Mr J. L. B. Matekoni instructed Mma Ramotswe in the ways of automatic gearboxes and helped her through the initial steps of starting and stopping such a vehicle. Then they left for a brief drive down the Tlokweng Road before doubling back and returning to the garage.

'It runs very sweetly,' said Mma Ramotswe as she finally drew to a halt beside the garage. 'And the ride is so smooth.'

Mr J. L. B. Matekoni beamed with pleasure. 'It will be a great change after your late van,' he said. She nodded her agreement. Yes, it would be a great change. Her late van, with all its quirks and noises, its unpredictability at times, its modesty and discomfort, was a world away from the

123

insulated, air-conditioned cocoon that was the driving cab of this new van. And although reliable transport was always a reassurance, and this new van was clearly reliable, the tiny white van was somehow more human, more like us, more natural than this gleaming construction of blue-painted metal.

Mr J. L. B. Matekoni was not entirely insensitive. 'I know,' he said quietly, laying a hand on her arm, 'I know that you will miss the old van. But you'll get used to this one soon, you know. And then it will become your new friend.'

She nodded grimly. Her pretence at cheerfulness and gratitude had slipped; she simply could not keep it up. 'I loved my tiny white van,' she stuttered. 'I loved it, you know.'

He looked down. 'Of course you did. You're a loyal lady, Mma Ramotswe, but machines come to the end of their lives, Mma—just like people. And I know it can be as hard to say goodbye to them as it is to say goodbye to people. I know that.'

They got out of the new blue van. Mma Ramotswe did not dare to look in the garage as she went back to the office. She did not want to see the tiny white van sitting there, alone, facing whatever fate it was that awaited machines that had served their purpose and now had no further work to do for us.

*   *   *

By the end of her first day at the Double Comfort Furniture Shop, Violet Sephotho had sold four beds. It was Phuti Radiphuti's practice to speak to the head of each department at a meeting convened immediately after closing time—to take a report on sales and to discuss delivery requirements for the following day. That afternoon had been a busy one, and there had been strong activity in the dining-room department, where two large tables and a dozen chairs had been sold between lunch time and the time of the sales meeting. In soft furnishings, a large leather sofa that had been slow to sell, and that was about to be discounted further, had suddenly been snapped up by a rather mousy man who had been brought in by his larger, domineering wife. That sale was the subject of warm congratulations by Phuti. 'We shall never stock a sofa that large again,' he said. 'The people in this country do not like big sofas like that. It is not the way we see things in Botswana.'

There had been murmurs of agreement on this. The sofa would not be missed, it was felt.

Then came the turn of the bed department. All eyes turned to Violet Sephotho, whose appointment, over the heads of one or two internal candidates, had been an unpopular one. There were those present who secretly wished her to have made no sales, which would have allowed them to mutter about the dangers of appointing an outsider who had no experience of selling furniture, even if she bore impressive credentials from other jobs.

'Four beds,' said Violet. 'I have sold only four beds. I shall try to sell more tomorrow—once I have got used to the job.'

The eyes that had been focused on Violet swivelled to Phuti Radiphuti.

'Four beds!' he said. 'That is very good, Mma! I would have been happy if you had sold two—or even one.'

Violet shrugged. 'It is not hard,' she said, and added, 'if you have the right skills.'

'Well, you certainly have those skills, Mma,' said Phuti. 'Four beds!'

One or two members of the staff looked away as this praise was heaped upon Violet; others smiled, even if their smiles were perhaps slightly fixed. And afterwards, when the sales meeting broke up, Phuti indicated to Violet that she should stay behind in his office.

'That is a very good effort,' he said. 'You have made a fine start, Mma.'

'Violet, please,' she corrected him.

'Yes, Violet. A very good effort.'

Violet made a self-deprecatory gesture—a small wave of the hand—to indicate that she thought such feats to be nothing special. Then, looking at her watch, she said, 'I must rush now, Rra. I have to be home soon to cook for my sick aunt. I am looking after her, you see, and she likes to have her meals on time.'

'Of course,' said Phuti. 'I do not want to keep you, Mma.' He hesitated. 'Would you like me to run you home, Mma . . . Violet? I was going to be leaving now anyway.'

Violet beamed at him. 'You're very kind, Mr Radiphuti.'

'Phuti, please,' said Phuti.

She nodded. 'Phuti, then. Yes, that would be very helpful. My poor aunt gets anxious.'

'Oh, I know how it is, Violet. When you're looking after an older relative. They are always worrying, worrying. This thing and then another thing. It can be a very great burden.'

126

'We do our best,' said Violet modestly, picking up her bag. 'It is not always enough, but we do it.'

Phuti locked the shop behind him and they got into his car. Violet sat demurely in the passenger seat, but her fingers wandered discreetly to touch the plush surface of the armrest beside her. And she took in, too, the expensive finish of the instrument panel.

'So you're cooking for your aunt,' said Phuti, as they drove off. 'I'm sure that you will be a good cook too.'

Violet basked in the pleasure of the *too*. Saleslady, lady of fashion, top-flight secretary . . . and cook. It was a litany of qualifications.

'I like cooking,' she said. 'And it is always an extra pleasure to be cooking for somebody else. It doubles the pleasure. Like your furniture gives double comfort.'

Phuti thought this very witty, and laughed enthusiastically.

Top-flight secretary, cook . . . and wit, Violet thought.

'Good cooking makes people happy,' said Phuti, adding, 'And it makes them full.'

He glanced away from the road at Violet and she realised that he had made a joke. She laughed loudly, and Phuti permitted himself a smile. This is going to be easier than I thought, Violet said to herself. Men. It was all so easy.

Phuti turned off on to the road that led past the Automotive Trades College. There was an intersection ahead, and beyond it a few craftsmen showed their wares under trees: roughly made chairs, some shapeless beanbags for sitting upon, pots of doubtful shape and usefulness. The traffic

127

was heavy as people made their way home, and Phuti, awaiting his turn to go through the intersection, found himself drawing up alongside a crowded minibus. It was not a sight to attract attention in any way; minibuses were everywhere, swaying along like overloaded boats, each a small, optimistic business, the pride of its proprietor. He did not look at this one, for there was nothing out of the ordinary to it, except for the fact that it carried, looking out of the window at that particular point, Grace Makutsi, assistant detective, on her way home from the No. 1 Ladies' Detective Agency.

Their eyes did not meet. Mma Makutsi, however, immediately recognised Phuti Radiphuti's car and gave a start. She sat bolt upright, face close to the window, taking in first the car, then Phuti at the wheel, and then, in an awful, heart-stopping moment, the figure of Violet Sephotho, false claimant of eighty per cent, writer of anonymous letters, Jezebel.

CHAPTER ELEVEN

BIG MAN TAFA

A Tuesday morning, thought Mma Ramotswe, is a good day on which to start work on a case. This was largely because of the positioning of Tuesday: Monday was a difficult day for no other reason than that it was Monday, the start of another week, with the prospect of another weekend as distant as it ever could be. Wednesday was halfway through the week, and a day on which, for some reason, there always seemed to be rather too much to do. By Thursday one was getting tired, and then on Friday, with the end in sight, one was in no mood to begin anything. That left Tuesday, which it now was; the day on which Mma Ramotswe found herself contemplating afresh the list of names of football players and deciding which of them to investigate first.

She glanced across the room at Mma Makutsi, who was sitting stiffly at her desk, in a way which Mma Ramotswe recognised as her bad-day posture. Mma Makutsi was like that; she could be moody, particularly when there was some problem on the domestic front. Certainly, there was something worrying her, but Mma Ramotswe knew better than to raise it with her at this point. It would come out later in the day, and she would be able to comfort or reassure her. Then the mood would lighten and everything would return to normal. That was what normally happened.

The Molofololo case was difficult not only because of the strange world of football with which it was concerned, but also because of the sheer challenge of looking into the private lives of quite so many men. She would have to delegate, she decided. Mma Makutsi could take on some of the names, Mr Polopetsi—if things were quiet in the garage—could be allocated a few of the others, and she would do the rest. Now, looking at the list, she picked up a pencil and divided the names. The drivers of the Mercedes-Benzes, each of whom had a tick against his name, were, according to Mr Polopetsi, unlikely candidates; they could be left to Mr Polopetsi himself in that case, as he was

129

the least experienced of the three of them. She then divided the remaining names at random between Mma Makutsi and herself.

She had decided that the best approach was to speak directly to the players. Mr Molofololo's suggestion that she pose as a masseuse was not practical, for a number of reasons. Prominent amongst these was that Mma Ramotswe had no idea of how to perform a massage, and she simply did not fancy pounding and manipulating the limbs of these muscly football players. She might pull the wrong way and make matters worse; she might tickle them inadvertently; anything could happen. No, that was not a good idea; far better to be transparent and to tell the players that she had been asked by Mr Molofololo to talk to everybody to find out what was going wrong. That had the benefit of being true, but it also gave people the chance to do what they liked to do best—which was to talk. Much as Mma Ramotswe admired Clovis Andersen's *The Principles of Private Detection*, it had to be said that this was one matter on which she felt she knew better than Mr Andersen himself. Nowhere in that great book did the author recommend the practice that Mma Ramotswe had found to be the strongest weapon in the private detective's armoury—that of asking people directly about something. That always worked, she found; always. When in doubt, ask somebody; it was as simple as that.

She looked at the list of names and the addresses beside them. She shook her head over the ridiculous football nicknames, smiling, though; men will be boys, she thought, especially when it comes to sporting matters. That was when men forgot their real age and went back to being ten or whenever it was that they were at their happiest. We all have a time, thought Mma Ramotswe—a time when the world was at its most exciting for us. Usually that time is somewhere in childhood, in that faded, half-remembered land that we all once dwelled in; that time of freshness and hope. For me it was . . . she stopped, and thought of Mochudi and the house she had lived in as a girl. And she saw her father, too, the late Obed Ramotswe, with his battered old hat that people laughed at but he loved so much. That was when I was happiest, she thought. Not that she was unhappy now—she was very happy; happy with her business, with her husband, with her tiny white . . . No, she was unhappy about that, but best not to think about it. Think of football instead and . . . Her eye moved down the list and came to Big Man Tafa. She would start there because she knew the road where he lived and also because she thought it would be a good idea to start with the goalkeeper. She remembered hearing people talking about him when they came out of the Stadium. Somebody had made a remark about his having been on the wrong side of the goal at the critical moment; not that she would have noticed that herself, but it was clearly obvious enough for somebody to remark on it—somebody who knew what he was talking about, as most people who attended football matches seemed to. There had been a lot of advice given to the players by the crowd; it had been a very well-informed crowd, Mma Ramotswe thought.

She looked across the room at Mma Makutsi. 'I am going to go to speak to one of these football

131

people,' she announced. 'I have divided the names on this list, and you might like to talk to some of them too.'

Mma Makutsi barely looked up from her desk. 'I do not see what is to be gained by talking to these people,' she muttered. 'They only like to talk about football.'

Mma Ramotswe was surprised at the degree of grumpiness in this answer, but she was patient. 'That's what we need to talk about in this case,' she said mildly. 'It is about football, you know.'

Mma Makutsi pouted. 'We will never find out anything from them,' she said. 'We won't have the faintest idea what they are talking about, Mma. Goals and lines and tackles and things like that. What is all of that about, Mma Ramotswe? That's what I ask you. What is that all about? What is this offside business? You hear men talking about it all the time. So-and-so was offside. No, he wasn't. Yes, he was. That sort of thing. What is the difference between that sort of language and Double-Zulu, Mma? That is the question.'

Mma Ramotswe looked at her assistant in astonishment. 'Double-Zulu, Mma? What language is that?'

Mma Makutsi waved a hand in the direction of the border. 'Something they speak somewhere over there. It is more difficult than Zulu. Twice as difficult. You cannot understand it. Nobody can.'

'Is there something worrying you, Mma?' asked Mma Ramotswe. 'You can speak to me about it— you know that.'

Mma Makutsi looked up now, her large glasses catching the sunlight slanting in through the small window behind Mma Ramotswe's desk; the lenses flashed like the eyes of an animal caught at night in the beam of a torch. 'Why do you think I am worried?' she snapped. 'I am sitting here working and you are talking about football, Mma. Forgive me, Mma, but it is not easy to work if somebody is talking about football all the time.'

Mma Ramotswe sighed. 'I'm sorry, Mma. I will try not to disturb you, but if you are unhappy, then please talk to me. It is not easy to be unhappy all by yourself, you know. It is easier if . . .'

She did not finish. Mma Makutsi had taken off her glasses and sunk her head in her hands. 'Oh, I am very unhappy, Mma,' she sobbed. 'And I am sorry that I have been accusing you of talking about football. You were not talking about football—it's just that I am a very unhappy lady, Mma.'

Mma Ramotswe quickly rose to her feet and crossed the room to Mma Makutsi's side. Bending down, she put her arms around her, feeling the heaving of her shoulders as the sobbing grew deeper.

'I could tell, Mma,' she said. 'I could tell that you were unhappy. What is it, Mma? Is it Phuti?'

The mention of Phuti Radiphuti's name brought forth a wail. 'It is, Mma. Oh, it is, Mma Ramotswe. I saw him. I saw him yesterday evening in his car.' She looked up at her employer. Tears ran down her cheeks, eroding the oily white cream that she rubbed each morning into her difficult complexion. Mma Makutsi wept cloudy tears as result, like milk.

Mma Ramotswe took her handkerchief and wiped at the tears. 'There, Mma. You've been wanting to cry. You saw Phuti in his car. Why be

133

upset about that?'

'In his car with Violet Sephotho,' said Mma Makutsi. 'That no-good woman. Temptress. She was smiling with that big, wicked smile of hers. She was like a leopard that has been hunting and is dragging her prey to her cave. That is what she looked like.'

Mma Ramotswe frowned. 'But you do not know why she was in the car?'

'She has gone to work for him,' said Mma Makutsi. 'Phuti has given her a job. She started yesterday and already she has her claws into him.'

Mma Ramotswe dragged a chair over to Mma Makutsi's side and sat down. 'Now listen, Mma. You must not jump to conclusions. Remember what Mr Andersen says? Remember that bit—I read it out to you once. He said *Do not decide that something is the case until you know it is the case.* Those were his exact words, were they not, Mma? They were. And if you apply them to this, all that you know is that for some reason— and you do not know what reason that is—Phuti had Violet Sephotho in his car yesterday evening. What time was it?'

'Oh, I don't know, Mma. Five thirty, maybe.'

'Five thirty? Well, what do people do at five o'clock, Mma? They go home, don't they?'

This brought a fresh wail from Mma Makutsi. 'He was taking her back home with him! Oh, Mma Ramotswe, that is what they were doing. They were going back to his house for immoral conversations.'

Mma Ramotswe made a dismissive sound. 'Nonsense, Mma. You have no evidence that anybody was thinking about immoral conversations, whatever those may be. What if Phuti was simply giving her a ride home—to *her* home—because she had stayed late in the store? What if that is all that he was doing? In fact, the more I think about it, the more I think that it is the most likely explanation. Don't you?'

Mma Makutsi did not, but after a few minutes of further comforting, she appeared to pull herself together. 'I must get on with my work, Mma Ramotswe,' she said. 'It is no good thinking about these things when I am trying to work. There will be time to think about them later.'

'You should talk about it,' said Mma Ramotswe. 'It is best to discuss these things, don't you think?'

Again, Mma Makutsi did not, and Mma Ramotswe decided that there was nothing further that she could do just then. It was time to go in search of Big Man Tafa, which she did, driving in her new, medium-sized blue van, that felt so alien, so wrong in every way.

Just as she was parking the van under a tree at the end of the street—a meandering, unpaved road of middle-range houses on the western edge of Gaborone—a small boy appeared. He was wearing a tiny pair of khaki trousers and a T-shirt several sizes too large for his spindly torso, had dust on his knees and a large sticking plaster across the bridge of his nose. And like all small boys who appear out of nowhere when one is looking for something, this one, she thought, would be bound to know in which of these houses lived Big Man Tafa. Small boys knew such things; they were familiar with the car number plates of every driver in the area; they knew the name of every dog associated with every house, and the vices of every such dog; they knew

135

the best place to find flying ants when the rains caused the termites to crawl up from their subterranean burrows and rise up into the sky, unless a small boy snatched them first, tore off their fluttering wings, and popped them, delicious morsels, into his mouth; they knew which trees harboured birds' nests and which did not; and which of the area's residents would pay you four pula to wash and polish the car.

The Principles of Private Detection contained no advice on the seeking of information from small boys, but Mma Ramotswe had often thought that it should. Perhaps she could write to Clovis Andersen one day and tell him of the things that were not in the book but that might appear in a future edition. But where was he, this Clovis Andersen, who knew so much about private detection? Somewhere in America, she imagined, because he sometimes mentioned famous cases in American cities that sounded so exotic to her ears that she wondered whether they really could exist. Where was this place called Muncie, Indiana? Or Ogden, Utah? Or, most intriguing of all, this town called Mobile, Alabama? Did that town move from place to place, as the name suggested? What happened there? Would they have heard of redbush tea, she wondered. Would they have heard of Gaborone?

'Big Man Tafa?' said the small boy in response to Mma Ramotswe's question. 'Yes, he lives here, Mma. He lives in that house over there. That one.'

He pointed a small, dirty finger in the direction of a house halfway down the street.

'In the yellow house?'

The boy nodded gravely. 'That is his house,

Mma. Mmakeletso lives there too.'

Mma Ramotswe smiled. The boy had used the traditional way of referring to a woman by naming her as the mother of her firstborn child. Mma Tafa, then, had a daughter called Keletso. That was an extra bit of information, which could be useful, but was probably not. There was more to come.

'She is a very fat lady,' said the boy, adding, politely, 'Like you, Mma.'

Mma Ramotswe patted him on the head. 'You are a very observant boy. And a good one, too. Thank you.'

She decided to leave the van where she had parked it and walk the short distance to the yellow house. The feel of a place—its atmosphere and mood—was often better absorbed on foot than from the window of a vehicle. She told the boy that if he watched her van, she would give him two pula when she came back. He was delighted, and scampered off to take up his post. A pity, she suddenly thought; if somebody stole my van, then I might get the old one back. An idle thought: it was too late for that.

She walked down the road towards the Tafa house. Most of the houses on the street had walls built about their yards, preventing a passer-by from seeing too much, but she was able to form a view of the neighbourhood in general. This was not a wealthy part of town, but it was not a poor one; it was somewhere in between. The people who lived here were halfway up the ladder: the deputy managers of the branches of banks—not quite full managers yet; civil servants who were senior enough to be able to imagine themselves, in ten

137

years' time perhaps, at a desk marked *Assistant Director*; deputy principals of schools. That, in itself, told her a lot before she even arrived at the gate of the Tafa house. This was a neighbourhood of people who were hoping to go up, but who were not yet where they wanted to be. And in the case of a goalkeeper, what did that mean? That he wanted to be captain, but was not yet in sight of it? What if you wanted to be captain and that post was taken? Your only hope in those circumstances would be for the captain to be got rid of—which presumably might happen if the team consistently lost over a period. Now that was an interesting thought, particularly if it came into the mind just as one walked down the short, cracked path that led from the gate to the front door of a goalkeeper's house.

*   *   *

Mma Tafa—or Mmakeletso—passed a cup of tea to Mma Ramotswe. They were sitting at the kitchen table, where Mma Tafa had invited Mma Ramotswe to join her.

'It is better for us to be in the kitchen, Mma,' said Mma Tafa. 'I am cooking a stew and I do not want it to spoil. If we sit there, then I can watch it.'

'I like to be in the kitchen,' said Mma Ramotswe. 'It is often the most comfortable room in the house. A sitting room can be too formal, don't you find, Mma?'

'I do, Mma. Our sitting room is often untidy. Big Man throws his newspapers down on the floor or leaves his shoes lying about. I am always picking things up in this house. All the time.'

Mma Ramotswe laughed. 'But men are always

138

like that. They need us, Mma. What would they do if we were not there to tell them where their clothes are? They would be walking around with no clothes on because they would not be able to find them.'

Mma Tafa gave a chortle. It was a strange laugh, thought Mma Ramotswe, rather like the sound of an elephant's stomach rumbling.

'You are very right, Mma,' said Mma Tafa. 'That would teach men to throw their clothes down on the floor. That would teach them.'

Mma Ramotswe took her tea cup gratefully. It was late morning, and very hot. There was a small fan on a shelf above the cooker but she noticed that its plug had been detached. Tea would be cooling. As she took her first sip, she noticed Mma Tafa's eyes upon her. She had told her host that she had been asked by Mr Molofololo to speak to his players to find out what was going wrong with the team. Big Man Tafa, his wife explained, was not in but would be back quite soon, in time for his lunch. Mma Ramotswe was welcome to stay until he arrived.

Mma Ramotswe sensed that Mma Tafa was glad of the company. She knew that it was not always easy for women in such places, where the easy companionship of the village had been replaced by the comparative anonymity of the town. Such a woman might spend much of the day without any contact with other women—an unnatural state of affairs, in Mma Ramotswe's view. We are born to talk to other people, she thought; we are born to be sociable and to sit together with others in the shade of an acacia tree and talk about things that happened the day before. We were not born to sit

139

in kitchens by ourselves, with nobody to chat to.

The absence of Big Man Tafa was convenient, as this would give Mma Ramotswe the chance to converse with his wife, and that, she knew, was often a better way of finding out about someone than talking to the person himself. So she lost no time in moving to the topic that had brought her to the kitchen of this yellow house.

'I do not think that the Kalahari Swoopers are doing all that well at the moment,' Mma Ramotswe said. 'That is a big pity, isn't it?'

Mma Tafa rolled her eyes upwards. 'It is very bad, Mma. When did the boys last win a game? I have almost forgotten.'

Mma Ramotswe looked into her tea cup. She did not want Mma Tafa to think that she was prying but she sensed that a few direct questions might yield valuable results. 'What's your view, Mma? Do you know why this is happening?'

She had chosen her words carefully. She had not asked Mma Tafa to tell her what Big Man Tafa himself felt, but she suspected that is what she would learn anyway.

And she was right. 'Big Man thinks that the problem is Mr Molofololo,' said Mma Tafa. 'He says that the boss doesn't know anything about football. He says this is always the problem with these rich men who own football teams. They think they can play, but they cannot.'

Mma Ramotswe listened intently. 'He does not like Mr Molofololo?'

Mma Tafa hesitated. 'I wouldn't say that.' She looked at Mma Ramotswe, uncertain as to whether to trust her; but trust won. 'No, maybe I would. Molofololo is very impatient, my husband thinks.

140

He says that he is always telling the players what to do. He says that this is the job of the coach, or the captain. But he says that the coach is weak and the captain used to be good, but no longer is. He says that the captain should go out to the cattle post and look after his cattle rather than trying to play football any more.'

The reference to cattle struck Mma Ramotswe as significant. Sooner or later, in any issue in Botswana, cattle nudged their way in, as they will nose their way into a feeding trough. It was as if in the resolution of any dispute, people had to ask themselves the question: What do the cattle think about this? She knew, of course, what cattle thought: cattle wanted rain, and the sweet green grass that rain brought, and apart from that they liked Botswana exactly as it was.

Mma Tafa looked at Mma Ramotswe's tea cup to see if it needed refreshing. 'Mind you, Mma,' she continued, 'it's interesting that Mr Molofololo gets somebody else to talk to his players about their problems. I mean no disrespect to you, Mma, but why ask a woman to go and speak to the men about football?'

Mma Ramotswe shrugged. 'Some people find it difficult to talk. Sometimes it's easier to get somebody else to talk for you.'

Mma Tafa let out a hoot of laughter. 'But that man is always talking! My husband says that he never stops. Do this, do that. Talking all the time.' She shook her head. 'No, the problem is that he cannot listen. That is his problem. So maybe he has chosen you to be his ears.'

Mma Ramotswe took her cue. 'And what do you think these ears should be hearing, Mma? What words would you like to put into those these ears?'

They understood one another perfectly. If there is a message, thought Mma Ramotswe, this will be it.

Mma Tafa stared at her. 'What words, Mma? Well, here is a message. *New captain*, Mma. That is the message. And if he says, where can I find a new captain, tell him that there is only one man who can do that job properly, and he is already on the team. Big Man. He should be the captain, Mma. And he cannot wait for ever. Soon. He must be the captain soon.' She paused. 'And your tea, Mma? Are you ready for another cup?'

Mma Tafa could not have made herself clearer, thought Mma Ramotswe. It was natural for a woman to feel ambition for her husband, but you could not always assume that this ambition was felt by the husband himself. Did Big Man Tafa really want to be captain, or was it a case of Mma Tafa wishing to be a captain's wife? She decided to ask the question directly. 'And Big Man?' she said. 'Would Big Man like to be in Rops's shoes?'

'I think so,' said Mma Tafa.

'You only think so, Mma? Have you not asked him?'

Mma Tafa sighed. 'Not all men know what they want to do, Mma. Many of them say that they are quite happy doing what they are doing, and do not know what they really want to do . . . underneath. You know what I mean, Mma?'

'I think I do,' said Mma Ramotswe.

'So it is the job of women—and that means you and me, Mma—to find out what our husbands *really* want to do, and then to tell them about it. That is our job, I think, Mma.'

Mma Ramotswe wondered about Mr J. L. B. Matekoni. He was a mild man—famously so—and she had never heard him speak about the things that he wanted to do. Did he have ambitions? He must at some time have wanted to have his own garage, and he must have worked towards the achieving of that goal. Then he had wanted to marry, and had proposed—eventually—which suggested that he must have nursed matrimonial ambitions. But apart from that, she wondered what unfulfilled desires lurked in his breast. Did he want to learn to fly a plane, as the owner of another garage had done? She thought not. He had been terrified on that occasion when Mma Potokwani had lined him up to do a charity parachute jump, and so it was unlikely that he wanted anything to do with aeroplanes. Did he want to learn to cook? Again, she thought not; Mr J. L. B. Matekoni had shown no interest in doing anything in the kitchen. Or did he want to go somewhere, perhaps to Namibia, to the sands and dunes of the coast down there, to the sea itself? He had never spoken of that.

The thought of Mr J. L. B. Matekoni nursing secret, unfulfilled ambitions saddened Mma Ramotswe, as did the thought of people wanting something very much indeed and not getting the thing they yearned for. When we dismiss or deny the hopes of others, she thought, we forget that they, like us, have only one chance in this life.

It was while Mma Tafa was filling the kettle for a second pot of tea, and while Mma Ramotswe was thinking of unfulfilled ambitions, that the kitchen door opened and Big Man Tafa came in. Seeing him up close, Mma Ramotswe was struck by the goalkeeper's diminutive stature—he seemed far smaller here in the kitchen, surprisingly so, than when standing in the goal. Of course it might have had something to do with his juxtaposition to Mma Tafa, who, beside her husband, seemed even larger than before. She positively flowed, thought Mma Ramotswe, flowed from a comfortable, cushiony centre to the outposts of her well-padded fingers; a great river of a woman. And he, the tiny goalkeeper, looked as if he might drown in the arms of such a wife; drown and be lost altogether. *Where is my husband?* Mma Tafa might say. *Has anybody seen him?* And they would reply: *In your arms, Mma, right there; be careful; he is right there, see.*

Introductions were made and Big Man sat down. When his wife explained that Mma Ramotswe was here on behalf on Mr Molofololo, a shadow crossed his face. He glanced at his wife, who responded with one of those looks that married couples can exchange; a look that conveyed far more than might any words. And then came the reassuring response that underlined the unspoken message: 'There is no trouble,' she said. 'Don't worry.'

Mma Ramotswe made a mental note of this comment. What trouble might Big Man Tafa expect from an emissary from Mr Molofololo? In one view, such a remark suggested that Big Man Tafa had reason to fear Mr Molofololo—and that, surely, is how a traitor to a football team might be expected to feel.

Big Man Tafa sat down opposite Mma Ramotswe at the table and listened attentively as she told him why she was there. 'Mr Molofololo

144

wants to hear what is wrong,' she said. 'That is why I am speaking to everybody.'

He relaxed visibly at the mention of everybody. 'Not just me?' he said.

'Of course not, Rra. Why would it just be you?'

She was aware of the sting at the end of her reply, and she watched his reaction carefully.

'Because when a goal is scored, it is always the goalkeeper who gets the blame,' he said. 'Always the poor goalie.'

That seemed understandable enough. And of course if anybody was in a position to give a match away, it was the goalkeeper.

Big Man Tafa clasped his hands together and settled back in his chair. 'You want to know what's wrong, Mma? I can tell you. Free. I can tell you free. Our captain—Rops Thobega. Have you met him?'

Mma Ramotswe shook her head. 'I met him briefly, Rra. I have not talked to him properly yet, Rra. But I will.'

Big Man wrinkled his nose. 'If he agrees to talk to you, that is. You will have to make an appointment, you know. The great Rops Thobega isn't one of those people you can just drop in on. Oh no. You have to phone and say to his wife, *Please may I speak to Rops, Mma? Not for long. Just one minute, please.* That's what you have to do.'

Mma Tafa laughed. 'And you have to make an appointment before you can speak to the wife. You have to phone up the maid and say, *Please, Mma, may I speak to Mma Thobega? Just one minute, etc. etc.*' She watched Big Man as she spoke, clearly taking pleasure from his approbation.

'That is very funny,' said Big Man. 'But

145

Mmakeletso is right. The whole lot of them have let his position go to his head. It is easier to speak to the President himself than it is to speak to him, I tell you!'

'That is not at all good,' said Mma Ramotswe. 'I think that you are telling me that the captain, this Rops, is no good.'

'I am,' said Big Man Tafa. 'And until he is replaced, then we are going to lose, lose, lose. I can tell you that, Mma.'

Mma Ramotswe looked thoughtful, weighing this information carefully. 'Tell me, Rra,' she asked, 'how do you replace a captain? Does this happen automatically if a team does very badly for a long time?'

She thought that they both hesitated, Mmakeletso and Big Man Tafa; she thought she saw them stiffen and look at each other. She waited.

'Oh, I don't know,' Big Man said after a while. 'It depends on the owner of the team. It will be up to Mr Molofololo, I suppose.'

Mma Ramotswe tried a different tack. 'Do you think it possible, Rra . . .' she began. 'Do you think it possible that somebody in the team might try to lose on purpose? Do you think that anything like that could happen?'

Big Man Tafa closed his eyes briefly. Then he opened them and stared at Mma Ramotswe in what looked like unfeigned horror. 'Never, Mma. You could tell, you see. Anybody could tell.'

Mma Ramotswe probed gently. 'How?'

Big Man Tafa tapped the table with his fingers. 'You can always tell when somebody is not doing his best. You can just tell.' He paused, as if

146

thinking of something for the first time. 'But now that you come to mention it, Mma, I think that there might be somebody not trying his best. Yes, I think I can say that.'

Mma Ramotswe watched him closely. His small frame, she thought, was like that of one of those creatures you see scurrying through the bush: wiry and difficult to catch. He would be a wonderful dancer, she decided. And then for a moment she pictured Big Man Tafa, dancing with his wife, lost in all that flesh, his dainty feet barely touching the ground as he was lifted up in her arms.

She tried to make the question sound unimportant—an afterthought. 'Who do you think is not trying his best?'

He answered immediately. 'Rops,' he said. 'If anybody wants us to lose, it must be Rops.'

She affected disbelief. 'Surely not, Rra. Surely not Rops. Why would he want that?'

'Because he hates Mr Molofololo,' said Big Man Tafa, 'and I believe that Mr Molofololo put Rops's brother-in-law out of business.'

'How did he do that?' Mma Ramotswe enquired.

Big Man did not know, but he assured Mma Ramotswe that it had happened and that Rops still felt angry about it.

'I see,' said Mma Ramotswe. 'But if Rops dislikes Mr Molofololo so much, why can he not just resign? He is such a well-known man that there will be many teams who will want him to play for them. He could go to Extension Gunners. He could go anywhere.'

Big Man Tafa shook his head. 'Rops is too old now. He can no longer play very well. Rops is finished.'

'But surely he wouldn't want to end his career like this,' Mma Ramotswe persisted. 'Who would want to retire after a long spell of losing every game?'

'Don't ask me,' said Big Man Tafa. 'You should know that sort of thing. You're the detective.'

Mma Ramotswe sat quite still. 'How do you know that, Rra? How do you know that I'm a detective?'

Big Man looked at her in surprise. 'Because everybody knows that, Mma Ramotswe. You are a famous lady in these parts. Mma Ramotswe of the No. 1 Ladies' Detective Agency. Everybody knows you now.'

'Your cover is blown,' said Mma Tafa, smiling at Mma Ramotswe. 'Isn't that what you detectives say?'

Big Man Tafa answered the question for her. 'It is,' he said.

*   *   *

As she walked back to the car, Mma Ramotswe was deep in thought. She was not quite sure what to make of her conversation with the Tafas; some things had become clearer while other things had become more obscure. Some things, indeed, were now quite unintelligible.

The small boy was sitting on duty at the van and she fished a couple of coins out of her bag to pay him.

'You have looked after the van very well,' she said, pressing the coins into his outstretched palm.

'Thank you, Mma.'

148

She looked down at him, at his funny, rather serious face; he was wiser perhaps than most boys of his age. *Boys know everything*, she remembered somebody saying. *Everything.*

'Tell me,' she said to the boy. 'Big Man Tafa: is he a good man, do you think, or is he a bad man?'

The boy's eyes moved slightly. A fly had landed on his head and was walking slowly across the smooth expanse of his brow. He did nothing to brush it off.

'He is bad man, I think,' he said. 'A very bad man. And one day God is going to punish him.'

Mma Ramotswe was taken aback. The judgement had been so swift, so clear; but it always is, she reflected, when you're that size.

'Who says he is a bad man?' she asked. 'Just you?'

The boy shook his head, making the fly take off from its suddenly uncertain landing strip.

'My father,' he said. 'Big Man Tafa owes my father ten thousand pula. That is this much, Mma.' He stretched out his hand to illustrate a pile of money. 'He says that only bad men don't pay what they have promised to pay. That is why I think that God will get him.'

Mma Ramotswe smiled. 'You are a very interesting boy,' she said.

CHAPTER TWELVE

CROCODILE SHOES

When Mma Ramotswe arrived back at an empty office, she found on her desk a handwritten note from Mma Makutsi:

Mma Ramotswe, I am feeling a bit better now and I have decided to go shopping. I need to think about the matter I discussed with you, but I must go to the shops now. Phuti is coming for dinner and I must buy food for him. I shall talk to him, Mma. You said that it is always best to talk and that is what I shall do.

Grace Makutsi, DSP

Mma Ramotswe smiled at this note. If the way we write a letter gives us away, as people said it did, then the DSP said it all: the Diploma in Secretarial Practice that Mma Makutsi had was her proudest possession—and understandably so. But did she have to put it after her name, and do so even when she wrote a note to her employer? Mma Ramotswe herself had no letters to put after her name, unless, of course, she wrote W, for Woman. Mma Precious Ramotswe, W. That seemed a bit unnecessary because the Mma made it clear that she was a woman, as did her first name, Precious. Perhaps she could put TBW (Traditionally Built Woman) or PI (Private Investigator). The last of these sounded much better, she thought, but really

150

was not necessary, as everybody appeared to know that she was a private detective, or so the Tafas had claimed.

She hoped that Mma Makutsi would handle her conversation with Phuti tactfully, and not say anything that she would later regret. When she had suggested to her assistant that she should talk about her concerns, Mma Ramotswe had not meant that she should talk to Phuti; she had meant that Mma Makutsi should talk to her. Discussing that sort of thing with a woman friend was one thing; discussing it with a man, and with the man under suspicion as well, was quite another, and much more hazardous. Men did not like to be suspected of unfaithfulness; indeed, she had heard of cases where men had responded to such accusations by going out and finding another girlfriend, even when there was no truth to the original accusation. It seemed that the mere mention of such a possibility could be enough to trigger the desire in a man's mind to do what he would otherwise not have done. One had to be extremely careful.

Mma Ramotswe thought it very unlikely that Phuti was entertaining the possibility of abandoning Mma Makutsi in favour of Violet Sephotho. Phuti had always struck her as being an unadventurous, loyal man; not the sort of man to take up with a woman like Violet, with her loud, loose ways and her utter ruthlessness. And yet, and yet . . . The problem was that men were weak, and sometimes the steadiest of men proved to be the weakest of all when faced with a determined onslaught. Violet probably knew that very well. She knew how to turn a man's head, as she would

151

have done so on many occasions before, presumably leaving a trail of broken engagements and marriages behind her. She was, Mma Ramotswe believed, a husband-stealer, as she had heard this accusation levelled against her on more than one occasion. And would Phuti, for all his fine qualities, be able to resist the devastating power of one so skilled in the sinister arts of husband-stealing?

She sat down at her desk, pondering these matters, and was doing this, looking up at the ceiling, when Fanwell came in.

'I know that it is not yet tea time, Mma,' he said, looking at his watch. 'But I am very thirsty. I would like to make some tea.'

'I am thirsty too,' said Mma Ramotswe. 'So perhaps you will make some for me, too.'

Fanwell went off to fill the kettle and returned a few moments later. While waiting for the water to boil, he sat on top of Mma Makutsi's desk, kicking his legs against the side. He would never have dared to do that, thought Mma Ramotswe, had Mma Makutsi been present, but he could be forgiven the presumption. There were some things that she herself did when Mma Makutsi was absent that she would never have dared to do in her presence—such as using her assistant's cup if her own cup needed washing and she was too busy—or it was too hot—to do it.

'I'm very sorry,' said Fanwell suddenly.

Mma Ramotswe looked up in surprise. 'What have you done?'

'No, I've done nothing, Mma. I'm very sorry about your late van.'

Mma Ramotswe sighed. 'You're very kind,

Fanwell. You're kind to say that.' Charlie, she had noticed, had said nothing about the end of her tiny white van, had even smiled over it, she recalled. But she was not vindictive, and there was no point in going into any of that.

'When we towed it away I felt very sad,' Fanwell went on. 'To think of all the times that van had carried you home and then back to the office. It must have been very sad for you, Mma.'

'It was,' said Mma Ramotswe. She had not seen the van being towed away, but it was no longer parked next to the garage and she assumed that the deed had been done. She hardly dared ask about the physical fate of the van, but now she decided that perhaps she should. She had counselled Mma Makutsi that it was best to talk; well, perhaps it was best for her to talk too, in her case about the van's fate.

She asked Fanwell what had happened, and he explained. 'We did it this morning,' he said. 'While you were away somewhere in your new van. The boss drove the truck and I steered your van. We took it to that man who finds spare parts from scrapped cars. Harry Moloso. He has that place in the industrial site, over that side. I sometimes go and get spares there. He is a fat man who drinks a lot of beer and has a stomach that goes out like this. That is where we took it.'

Mma Ramotswe listened to this with a growing feeling of emptiness. It was not a dignified end for her tiny white van—to be handed over ignominiously to Harry Moloso with his beer belly and his oxyacetylene torch waiting in the background, every bit the cruel instrument of torture. She shuddered.

153

Fanwell whistled. 'It's a pity about your van, Mma,' he said. 'Maybe it could have been fixed after all. If one could find the parts. A big job, though.'

Mma Ramotswe was silent, and Fanwell looked at her, smiling. 'Very big job. But there must be some of them somewhere. If you looked hard enough.'

Mma Ramotswe took a pencil in her hand and played with it gently between her thumb and forefinger. 'Parts?'

'Yes,' said Fanwell. 'You'd need to get . . . Oh, it's a long list, Mma. Not worth doing, which is what the boss said when we opened it up. He's right, I think.'

It was the smallest of straws, but a straw none the less. 'But it could be done? You could find the parts somewhere, do you think?'

Fanwell nodded. 'You'd start at Harry Moloso's. He must have had vans like that going through. He must have some of the parts. And Harry Moloso knows everybody in the parts business, Mma. He can phone Johannesburg if necessary and speak to somebody there. Or Francistown, Mafikeng—anywhere. He has the contacts.' He smiled. 'Me—I have no contacts. None.'

Mma Ramotswe looked down at her desk. Was it worth it? She loved that van, and although the new van was very comfortable and efficient, were comfort and efficiency the only things in this life? She thought they were not. If they were, then would she and Mma Makutsi be doing what they were now doing, working for very little money in a funny little office next to a garage? She could get a far more comfortable job, she thought, and Mma

154

Makutsi had Phuti to look after her—if she still had him, that is—and she would soon have no need to work. No, comfort was not the only thing. They worked in the No. 1 Ladies' Detective Agency because they wanted to help people with the problems in their lives. And they sat in these old chairs because they had always sat in them and they felt loyal to the things that had served them well. The tiny white van had served her well, and it had been towed off to Harry Moloso's scrapyard; that had been its reward.

She looked up at Fanwell, who was watching her, a smile playing at the edges of his mouth. She took a deep breath. 'Do you think . . .' she began.

The apprentice had anticipated her question. 'Yes,' he said. 'I could try.'

She let out her breath. 'Can we go round there some time? Not today, but some time soon?'

Fanwell made a gesture that implied that whatever Mma Ramotswe wanted to do would be convenient to him. 'I can't guarantee anything, Mma Ramotswe,' he said.

'Who can guarantee anything?' asked Mma Ramotswe in reply.

Fanwell laughed. 'Your sign out there says satisfaction guaranteed, docsn't it? *The No. 1 Ladies' Detective Agency—Under Personal Supervision—Satisfaction Guaranteed.*'

'I suppose, that is, we'd *like* to guarantee,' said Mma Ramotswe. She felt that she wanted to get up and hug this young man but she could never do that. She imagined for a moment hugging him and then Mma Makutsi coming back into the office and misinterpreting what she saw. She would have to say, *But I was just hugging him for sheer joy,*

155

Mma, and Mma Makutsi would tactfully say, *Of course, Mma, of course.*

*   *   *

At the time that Fanwell and Mma Ramotswe were having their conversation about the tiny white van, Mma Makutsi was at the River Walk shops, walking through the concourse that led to the supermarket. The shops on either side of her were all tempting in their various ways—except for the outdoor clothing shop, for which she had no time at all. She had no interest in bush clothing—all those ridiculous jackets with too many pockets and slouch hats and so on. She did not like the bush very much; she was prepared to accept that there were some who did, but Mma Makutsi was one for urban comforts. There were things in the bush that could bite one—and did, if they had the chance. And of course if one ventured into the real bush, the remote tracts of land that stretched out to the northern reaches of the country, the great plains and the mopani forests, there were creatures that could make a person feel very uncomfortable indeed. Mma Makutsi knew about this because one of her forebears, her grandfather on her mother's side, had been attacked by a lion outside Maun. He was a driver for a company that carted provisions from Francistown to the Delta, and he had stopped en route in a small village where he had a cousin. As he prepared to leave before dawn, he had been set upon by a large lioness that had mauled him badly, before the villagers, hearing his screams, had come out brandishing sticks. Mma Makutsi had been deeply affected by this story

156

when she was a small girl, and had been nervous of the bush since then.

Of course there was no danger of lions in Gaborone, in the River Walk shopping centre, but who knew what lurked just beyond the edge of the town? The dam was not far away, after all, and beyond the dam there was a stretch of country where great antelopes might be seen—kudu and eland—and if they were there, then why should there not be the creatures that preyed on them— lions and leopards? And were there not crocodiles in the dam, no matter what people said about there being none? Crocodiles . . . She stopped. The supermarket was just round the corner but here, at her right hand, was the window of a shoe shop, and there, on a small display stand, was a pair of what looked like crocodile-leather shoes.

Mma Makutsi stopped to peer through the window. It was difficult to tell with leather—the shoes at the front of the display were definitely ostrich skin, one could see that from the tiny bumps—but those on the stand had a very different texture. Could they be hippo skin? Surely not. She had never heard of hippo hide being used to make shoes and she doubted whether it would appeal very much. She could not imagine herself saying, *These are my new hippo-hide shoes*; that conveyed entirely the wrong impression. Perhaps Mma Ramotswe could wear hippo-hide shoes; perhaps it was just the right leather for the shoes of traditionally built people.

She hesitated. She had not come to the shopping centre to buy shoes; she had come to buy food, and there was a big difference between shopping for food and shopping for shoes, a difference concentrated in one word: *guilt*. There was no guilt at all in buying day-to-day requirements, such as food, whereas the purchase of shoes, even shoes that were intended for working use, was a process very susceptible to the onslaughts of conscience. Were the shoes necessary? Were shoes *like this* necessary? Would anybody believe that such shoes could possibly have been bought with functionality in mind? Such were the questions that confronted Mma Makutsi every time she entered a shoe shop. And such were the questions that she resolutely, and with admirable determination, swept aside before making a purchase.

Her hesitation was not long-lived. There would be plenty of time to buy the food for dinner even if she went into the shoe shop now. And she did not necessarily have to go in to *buy*; it was perfectly possible to go into a shoe shop just to look, even if Mma Makutsi inevitably came out with a new pair of shoes. This time it would be pure curiosity about the crocodile-skin shoes, nothing more than that.

The assistant recognised her. Her sister had been at the Botswana Secretarial College at the same time as Mma Makutsi; indeed, they had been quite good friends. 'Mma Makutsi,' she said as she sidled up. 'We haven't seen you for some time. Are you well, Mma?'

'Thank you, Mma. I am very well. And you are well?'

'I am well too, Mma. Thank you.'

There was a silence. Then Mma Makutsi continued, 'And your sister is well too?'

'She is. She has had another baby. And the baby is well.'

'That is good.'

The silence returned. Mma Makutsi glanced in the direction of the window. 'I couldn't help noticing, Mma,' she said, 'that you had a very smart pair of shoes in the window there. Those ones on the stand. They are very pretty shoes.'

The assistant laughed. 'They are, Mma. They are very pretty. And that's why we put them on that stand—so that if you walked past you would see them. And you have.'

She moved over towards the window and leaned forward to take the shoes off the stand. Returning to Mma Makutsi, she held them out in front of her, like a prize. 'There, Mma. Look at those. These are very fine shoes.'

Mma Makutsi reached forward and took one of the shoes from the assistant's hand. She turned it over and examined the heel and the sole. The heel was high, but not so high as to make the shoes impractical. She looked inside: the workmanship was impeccable; neatly stitched seams ran down the side of the leather lining, and everything was meticulously and expertly finished. She ran a finger over the leather; it felt just right.

'They were made in Johannesburg,' said the assistant. 'These shoes are exactly the style being worn today in Johannesburg, by the very fashionable ladies there. You know that, of course.'

Mma Makutsi nodded. 'Of course.'

'But they are now being worn in Gaborone too,' went on the assistant. 'By our own more fashionable ladies.'

Mma Makutsi sat down silently on one of the chairs while the assistant, having given her the other shoe, fetched small nylon socks. The decision to try the shoes had been made wordlessly, but everything was well understood. The assistant knew what was going on in Mma Makutsi's mind and would leave her to conduct the internal struggle by herself; no help was needed from her. Other than to remark, perhaps, that the shoes were made of a leather which looked very like crocodile, but which was not. It was crocodile-look, apparently, which was not the same thing. 'It is better for the crocodiles,' explained the assistant. 'And it is just as beautiful. Many people would think that you are wearing crocodile if they saw those shoes. That is what they would think, Mma.'

Mma Makutsi slipped the shoes on to her feet. They were exactly the right size and fitted perfectly. She glanced at the assistant who nodded encouragingly. She stood up.

'I am not sure when I would wear these shoes,' she said as she took a tentative step.

The assistant spread her hands. 'Oh, Mma, you could wear them to all sorts of parties. They are ideal party shoes.'

Mma Makutsi looked down at the shoes. 'I do not go to many parties,' she said. 'In fact, I go to none.' This was true. Mma Makutsi was not a party-goer and Phuti had never so much as suggested going to one.

'Or not,' the assistant added hurriedly. 'These shoes do not need to go to parties. You can wear these to work. When you are entertaining a client. Or even for ordinary wear—when you feel that you want to look smart, even if you are doing nothing special. You could wear these shoes all the time, you know.'

'They are very pretty,' said Mma Makutsi. 'Very

elegant.'

The assistant nodded. 'That is what I thought when I first saw them. I thought that these are the most elegant shoes we have had in the shop for a long time.'

Mma Makutsi asked the price. It was steep, but then she told herself: I am the fiancée of a wealthy man—still—and he has often said that he would buy me shoes and clothes. And I have never taken advantage of that; never. She looked into her purse. She had been to the bank to draw money and there was just enough for the shoes, even if nothing would be left over for the food.

It was a stark choice: shoes or food; beauty or sustenance; the sensible or the self-indulgent.

'I'll take these shoes,' she said firmly.

The assistant smiled broadly. 'You'll never regret it, Mma,' she said. 'Never. Not once.'

*   *   *

Mma Makutsi caught a minibus home. She was empty-handed, apart from the shoes, which had been placed in their elegant box and then in a plastic carrier bag. This bag sat on her lap where, had she not thrown caution to the winds, her shopping bag of groceries would have been. But had she bought groceries, she would not be experiencing that extraordinary feeling of renewal that an exciting purchase can bring. And did she really need groceries? There were some potatoes at home, and some spinach. There were also a couple of eggs and some bread. With a little ingenuity, what food there was could be combined to produce a tasty enough morsel for Phuti

Radiphuti's dinner—a potato and spinach omelette perhaps, or fried egg and chips, a simple meal, but one which was exactly the sort of thing that men liked to eat.

She alighted from the minibus and walked the short distance to her house. Once inside, she sat down on one of the chairs at her table and took off her old shoes. Then, standing up, she walked around the room in the new shoes. The old shoes watched, looking at her reproachfully: *Off with the old and on with the new, Boss*, they said. *So much for loyalty.*

She shook her head. She would not be throwing the old shoes away; they should know that. *You are still important to me*, she said.

The shoes said nothing. They were sceptical,

The new shoes, once on, looked proudly at the old shoes. *Eat your heart out, old ones,* they said. *You're history.*

They are not, thought Mma Makutsi. They are not history. There's a place for all sorts and conditions of shoe.

Yeah, Boss, said the old shoes. *Kind words, but the bottom line is this: we're history. Well, you'd better look out, Boss! What if you're history yourself?*

She sat down again. The shoes, both old and new, were silent. Shoes cannot talk, she thought; it's just me talking to myself.

History, whispered the old shoes.

She looked down. The shoes, lying on the floor, were silent, their tongues loose, mere scraps of leather really, but with the look of self-satisfaction that came from having issued a well-timed and much-needed warning.

CHAPTER THIRTEEN

HOW WE WORRY

'I am going now,' said Mr J. L. B. Matekoni, standing at the kitchen door the following morning. 'It's a Lobatse day.'

'Of course,' said Mma Ramotswe. She had forgotten, but was now reminded, that this was one of the days when Mr J. L. B. Matekoni went to help a friend who owned a garage in Lobatse. This friend, who had recently bought the business, was struggling to cope after an employee's premature retirement. Mr J. L. B. Matekoni had stepped into the breach, offering to spend a day every two weeks—taking Charlie with him—helping to get through the backlog of work. It was typical of him, thought Mma Ramotswe fondly, that he should come to the rescue in this way. But inevitably there was more work than he and Charlie could manage, and the Lobatse days were long ones.

'I'll try to be back in time for my dinner,' said Mr J. L. B. Matekoni. 'But you know how it is.'

Mma Ramotswe did know. He would not be back until ten that night, perhaps even later, and she would worry about him until she saw the lights of his truck at the front gate. That journey could be perilous at night, what with bad drivers and with animals straying on to the road. She knew of so many people who had collided with cattle at night; one moment the road was clear and then, with very little or no warning at all, a cow or a donkey would nonchalantly wander out in front of the car. But

163

you could worry too much about these things, thought Mma Ramotswe, and she knew that worrying about things was no help at all. Of course you were concerned for those you loved; it would be impossible not to be so. She worried about Motholeli; about the sort of future that lay ahead for a girl in a wheelchair. It helped if such a girl was as plucky as Motholeli, but would pluck be enough to get her through the disappointments that must surely lie ahead? What if she wanted to marry and have a family? Would there be a young man ready to take on the responsibility of a handicapped wife? And Mma Ramotswe was not even sure whether it would be possible for Motholeli to have a child, even if there was a husband to hand. She had not really given it much thought, but the time would come when she would have to do so.

And Puso, what about him? He was a strange boy—a little bit distant, which was to be expected, perhaps, from a child who had had such a difficult start in life. She felt now that they were getting through to him, but sometimes she wondered how he would turn out. Had he been the natural son of Mr J. L. B. Matekoni, then she might have said that Mr J. L. B. Matekoni's gentle breeding would come through; but he was not, he was the son of a man whom they would never know anything about.

Such doubts were only to be expected, and it would be strange if foster-parents never thought of these things. Yet there was no point in allowing niggling doubts to flower into consuming worries. The important thing was to get on with life and to give the children the love they deserved. She did that, and she knew that in their hearts they loved

164

her back.

As she watched Mr J. L. B. Matekoni walk out to his truck that morning, Mma Ramotswe felt herself overcome by a sudden feeling of vulnerability, by a fear that her familiar world was hanging by a thread. We were tiny creatures, really; tiny and afraid, trying to hold our place on the little platform that was our earth. So while the world about us might seem so solid, so permanent, it was not really. We were all at the mercy of chance, no matter how confident we felt, hostages to our own human frailty. And that applied not only to people, but to countries too. Things could go wrong and entire nations could be led into a world of living nightmare; it had happened, and was happening still. Poor Africa; it did not deserve the things that had been done to it. Africa, that could stand for love and happiness and joy, could also be a place of suffering and shame. But that suffering was not the only story, thought Mma Ramotswe. There was a story of courage and determination and goodness that could be told as well, and she was proud that her country, her Botswana, had been part of that.

Before getting into the truck Mr J. L. B. Matekoni turned and waved. She waved back from the window and suddenly, inexplicably, felt an urge to rush out into the yard to speak to him before he left, to tell him something. She stood quite still; the urge was a strong one, but there was a part of her that said that she should not be silly, that she should stay where she was. She was holding a kitchen towel in her hand and found herself twisting it in her anxiety. Now she flung it aside and made for the door.

165

He had started his truck and was reversing down the driveway. When she appeared round the side of the house he spotted her and waved again, thinking that she was on her way out to the garden. But then he saw that she was waving to him as if she had forgotten to tell him something, some message, no doubt, about picking up something from the shops in Lobatse before he came home. There was a butcher there who was a distant relation of Obed Ramotswe and gave them good cuts of meat at a special price. It would be about that, he thought.

Mr J. L. B. Matekoni wound down his window. 'Yes, Mma Ramotswe,' he said. 'I'll go to the butcher. What do we need this time?'

She shook her head. He saw that she was looking at him intently, as if she were expecting a message or waiting for him to say something.

'What is it, Mma Ramotswe?'

She shook her head. 'I don't know, Mr J. L. B. Matekoni. I suppose I just wanted to say something to you. And now I don't really know what it is.'

He began to smile, and was on the point of chiding her for being forgetful, when he stopped. There was something in her demeanour that suggested concern; it was almost as if she were frightened; as if she wanted to be reassured by him. He reached out of the window and touched her arm gently, then took her hand in his, awkwardly, as his position inside the cab of the truck did not make it easy. 'What is it, Mma Ramotswe? Is there anything wrong?'

She answered no, there was nothing wrong. Did he know how sometimes you felt horribly anxious;

you felt that something was going to happen? He thought about that for a moment; yes, he understood that feeling, but nothing bad was going to happen. And then he asked her whether she was upset about her van. She shook her head to that.

'Then what is it?'

She gave his hand a squeeze. 'I wanted to thank you,' she said.

He was puzzled. 'For what? Thank me for what?'

'For everything that you've given me, Mr J. L. B. Matekoni.'

He looked away. He was not one for displays of emotion; he never had been, but it made his heart swell to be thanked by this woman who stood for so much in his eyes; who stood for kindness and generosity and understanding; for a country of which he was so proud; who stood for Africa and all the love that Africa contained.

'I am the one who should say thank you, Mma Ramotswe,' he said. 'You are the one who has given everything.'

She gave his hand a last, fond squeeze and then stood back. 'I mustn't hold you up,' she said. 'Lobatse.'

He sighed. 'Yes, Lobatse.'

He put the truck into gear and she watched him drive out on to the road. In the background, she heard the neighbour's dogs start to bark at the sound of the truck's engine. Those dogs, she thought; they lay in wait for anything that passed, human or mechanical, ready to defend their tiny patch of territory against whatever incursion, as do we all.

It had been a very unsettling feeling but she had largely recovered from it by the time she herself left the house half an hour later. The children had been dispatched to school, Puso pushing Motholeli's wheelchair for the short journey. He was old enough to do that now, and did it without complaint; it was lodged in his mind somewhere, thought Mma Ramotswe, that his sister had looked after him, had saved his life, in fact, when he was very small. He did not remember that, of course, but he had been told about it, and he knew.

She drove down Zebra Drive in her new van. There were no mysterious, unidentifiable rattles as there had been in the old van, nor bumps as she drove over parts where the road surface had been inexpertly repaired. All was smoothness, like being in a canoe, a *mokoro*, on the untroubled waters of the Okavango. For many people, that would have been perfect, but not for Mma Ramotswe. One could go to sleep in such a van, she thought, as one was driving along. It was not unlike being in bed.

For a few moments she felt herself becoming drowsy, and had to blink and shake her head to wake herself up, such was the power of auto-suggestion. I must not think such thoughts, she told herself; it was just like those occasions when one thought of doughnuts and immediately became hungry. Doughnuts. And in the pit of her stomach she felt a sudden pang of hunger, even though it was less than an hour since she had enjoyed a good breakfast of maize porridge and slices of bread spread thick with apricot jam. Apricot jam . . . The hunger pangs returned.

Mma Makutsi was already in the office when Mma Ramotswe arrived.

'There is a lady,' she said, nodding in the direction of the garage. 'She is out there at the side. She would not come in.'

Mma Ramotswe frowned. Had she forgotten that somebody was coming, or had Mma Makutsi made an appointment without telling her?

It was as if Mma Makutsi had read her mind. 'She has no appointment. She just turned up.'

People sometimes turned up; it was not unusual. They saw the sign and came to take a closer look. Sometimes they were shy and stood under the tree for a while, plucking up the courage to go into the office. Mma Ramotswe was always reassuring to such people. 'You must not be ashamed,' she said. 'Anybody can need a private detective—even a private detective.'

She settled herself behind her desk. 'You may fetch her, Mma. Tell her that I am here.'

She glanced at her desk and pushed a few papers to the middle. A tidy desk might create a good impression in the eyes of some but a desk that was quite bare could send quite the wrong message. Not that this was likely to be a client who would need impressing; a woman who came on foot and who was shy about waiting inside was unlikely to be the sort of client who would notice these things.

Mma Makutsi brought her in.

'*Dumela*, Mma,' said Mma Ramotswe, Good morning, and reached out to shake the woman's hand. '*O tsogile jang?*' How are you?

Her greeting was returned. '*Ke tsogile sentle, wena o tsogile jang?*' I am fine, and how are you?

169

Mma Ramotswe gestured for her visitor to sit down, and as she did so she realised where she had seen this woman before. She had looked familiar; now she knew. 'You and I have met before, haven't we, Mma?'

The visitor inclined her head. 'We have, Mma. That morning. You were walking to work.'

'Yes. I remember.'

There was silence. Mma Ramotswe waited a few moments before she spoke. 'I said to you, Mma, that you could come and speak to me. I am glad that you have come.'

The woman looked up, surprised. 'Why?'

'Why am I glad that you have come?' Mma Ramotswe spread her hands. 'Because that is why we're here, Mma. It is our job to help people. That is what we do.'

The woman looked uncertain and Mma Ramotswe added, gently, 'We do not want your money, Mma. We help everyone. You do not need to pay.'

'Then how do you eat, Mma?' asked the woman.

Mma Ramotswe smiled. 'As you can tell, Mma, I am not one who does not get enough food. We eat because there are some rich people who come to us. They pay us. Rich people can be very unhappy, you know, Mma.'

The woman did not look as if she believed this. 'Rich people must be very happy, Mma.'

Mma Ramotswe glanced at Mma Makutsi, who had settled herself back at her desk and was following the conversation with interest.

'What Mma Ramotswe says is true,' Mma Makutsi interjected. 'We have many rich people who come into this office and sit where you are sitting, Mma, in that very chair, and cry and cry, Mma. I'm telling you. Many tears—many, many tears.'

Mma Ramotswe thought this a bit of an exaggeration but did not contradict her assistant. There were people who cried in the office—that was only to be expected when people were discussing their problems—but not all of these were rich and they generally did not cry quite the volume of tears implied by Mma Makutsi.

Mma Ramotswe sat back in her chair. 'So, Mma, you are here now and we are here too. I think this would be a good time for us to talk. You must not be afraid of talking to us.'

'We tell nobody,' chipped in Mma Makutsi. 'You need not worry about that.'

The woman nodded. 'I know that,' she said. 'Somebody told me that you people are like priests. They said that a person can tell you anything, and you will not talk about it.'

Mma Ramotswe was patient, but in the ensuing silence she glanced discreetly at her watch. She wondered whether a priest was what this woman needed; on occasion, people came into the office simply because they needed to unburden themselves of some secret. She listened, of course, to these people and she felt that it probably helped. But often she was unable to provide the thing that they needed: forgiveness. She could point them in the right direction for that, but she could not provide it. She had a feeling that this was one of those cases.

'There is something troubling you, Mma, isn't there? Something you have done?'

The woman stared at the floor. 'Something I

have done?' Her voice was flat—without salience. 'No, Mma. It is something I am doing.'

Mma Ramotswe said nothing. At the other side of the room she saw Mma Makutsi watching, her large glasses catching the morning light from the windows.

She probed gently. 'Something you are still doing? A bad thing?'

The woman moved her head so slightly that it would have been easy to miss the acknowledgement. 'I did not think about it,' she said quietly. 'I did not think about it at all. It just happened.'

Mma Makutsi leaned forward at her desk. It was difficult for her, with the client's chair facing Mma Ramotswe, and she always found herself addressing the back of the client's head, as she did now. But it gave her a certain advantage, she found, to speak from behind somebody; it was like interrogating a person under a strong light. Clovis Andersen disapproved of that, of course. *Never use third-degree methods*, he wrote. *It does not get to the truth*. What was this third degree? Mma Makutsi wondered. And what were the first and second degrees? Were they worse, or in some way better?

'You did not know what you were doing, Mma?' she prompted. 'Or you did not know that what you did was bad?'

Mma Ramotswe gave Mma Makutsi a discouraging look.

'Mma Makutsi is just trying to help,' she said.

The woman looked anxiously over her shoulder. 'I do not know, Mma,' she said. 'I am not an educated woman.'

Mma Ramotswe spoke soothingly. 'That is not

important, Mma. There are many people who have not had an education who are very clever people indeed. It is not their fault that they have not been to school.'

'People laugh at people like me,' said the woman. 'These days, when everybody is so educated.'

'If they laugh at you, then they are fools themselves,' said Mma Ramotswe. 'Big fools.' She paused. 'But, Mma, you must tell me what is making you unhappy. What is this thing?'

The woman looked up and met Mma Ramotswe's gaze. 'I am a lady with two husbands,' she said. 'That is me.'

There was a sound from the back of the room—a form of hissing from Mma Makutsi—an exhalation, really, not a hiss of disapproval. 'Two husbands,' she muttered.

The woman sighed. 'I do not approve of women who have two husbands,' she said. 'But now I am one myself.'

Mma Ramotswe frowned. 'It is against the law, you know, Mma, to get married twice. You do know that, don't you?'

The woman looked surprised. 'Oh, I am not married,' she said. 'These men are just boyfriends. But they are very good ones. They are like husbands. I call one my weekday husband and the other my weekend husband.'

Mma Ramotswe looked up at the ceiling. What could she do? People treated her like one of those agony aunts in the newspapers—they expected her to make their decisions for them. This woman was obviously troubled but she did not see what she could do for her, other than advise her to give one boyfriend up. But presumably other people would have told her that, and she expected something more from her and Mma Makutsi.

'Choose,' said Mma Makutsi. 'Choose one of them.'

'That is not easy,' said the woman.

Mma Makutsi laughed. 'No, it never is. But you have to, Mma. You cannot have two husbands. You will be punished for that one day. One of them will find out about the other, and then you will be finished.'

This brought a sharp reprimand from Mma Ramotswe. 'Mma Makutsi!' It did not help if the assistant detective said to the client that she would be finished. It was unprofessional.

'I am only telling her the truth, Mma,' Mma Makutsi protested.

Unexpectedly, the woman sided with Mma Makutsi. 'Yes,' she said. 'You are right, Mma. I will be finished big time—and very soon. I have a very big problem—one of the husbands has gone to work for the other in his business. It is a very small business—just three men. Now one husband—the weekend husband—says that he wants to invite the other husband to have dinner at our house. He asked me to cook for them.' She paused, watching Mma Ramotswe, who was staring at her in anticipation. 'And the second husband—the one who has been invited—has now asked me to come with him to this dinner. I will be the lady cooking for that dinner, in the house of my other husband.'

'You see!' broke in Mma Makutsi. 'You see where lies and cheating get you, Mma? You see!'

'Thank you, Mma Makutsi,' said Mma Ramotswe. She quickly went over possibilities in

174

her mind. People got themselves into the most uncomfortable situations, and one could not always rescue them. She could not take on the emotional problems of all Gaborone, much as she would like to help. No, she would have to get this woman to shoulder responsibility for the fix she had created for herself. 'Now, Mma, I'm very sad that you find yourself in this unhappy position. I would love to be able to solve it for you, but what can anybody do? Some problems we have to solve ourselves—and this is one of them.'

From the other side of the room came Mma Makutsi's verdict. 'Yes.'

'You are going to have to speak to these men,' Mma Ramotswe continued. 'That is all you can do. I cannot solve this problem for you, you know. I'm very sorry but I cannot.'

The woman looked crestfallen. 'Oh, Mma Ramotswe, I'm so frightened . . .'

'Frightened?'

'Yes, I'm frightened of what these men will do. You know how angry men can become.'

Mma Ramotswe did. For a moment she saw her first, abusive husband, Note Mokoti. She saw his hand raised. She saw the anger in his eyes.

'I have an idea,' said Mma Makutsi.

They both turned to look at her. She was smiling—with the air of one to whom a sudden revelation has come.

'Speak to both of them,' said Mma Makutsi. 'Separately, of course. Tell each husband that you have been weak and have been seeing another man. Then ask each man to forgive you.'

The woman started to protest. 'But how . . . ?'

Mma Makutsi raised a finger. 'Watch their

reactions very closely, Mma. See how they behave. They will probably behave differently. Watch them and then choose the one who is prepared to forgive you the most. That one will be the kind one. Choose to stay with him and say to the other that you are sorry but you cannot stay with him.'

For a while nobody spoke. Outside in the garage, Fanwell and Mr Polopetsi were hammering on metal. Fanwell said something and a peal of laughter drifted through the door.

The woman stared at Mma Ramotswe and then turned round and smiled at Mma Makutsi. 'That is a very good idea, Mma. That is very wise.'

Mma Makutsi looked down modestly. 'I am glad that you think so, Mma.'

'And so do I,' said Mma Ramotswe. 'I think that even Sherlock Holmes would be proud of that suggestion.'

'Who is this Rra Holmes?' asked the woman.

'He was a very famous detective,' said Mma Ramotswe. 'Over that way.' She waved a hand in the direction of north. 'He lived in London. He is late now.'

'I will do what you have suggested,' said the woman. 'My heart is lighter now.'

'Good,' said Mma Ramotswe. 'And come back and let us know what happens, Mma . . .' She broke off. She realised that she did not know the woman's name and now it had become obvious. That was the trouble when everybody could be addressed as Mma or Rra; sometimes one did not get the name at the beginning and then it became embarrassing to ask for it.

'My name is Mma Sephotho,' said the woman. 'Lily Sephotho.'

*   *   *

'Well!' expostulated Mma Makutsi after Mma Sephotho had left. 'What can I say, Mma? I do not know. I do not know.'

It was rare for Mma Makutsi to profess speechlessness; indeed it had never happened. Her declaration of speechlessness, however, was accompanied by a flood of words, all of them expressing a mixture of astonishment and its opposite: she was astonished but not astonished—if Violet Sephotho was to have a mother, then her mother surely would be exactly the sort to have two husbands. Not that they were real husbands, of course: nothing quite so respectable as that in a household of loose women. Two men—that is what Mma Sephotho had—two men. And by her own admission—in her own so very apt words—these were a weekday man and a weekend man. Had Mma Ramotswe ever heard these matters put so crudely? And had the woman not talked about it as shamelessly as one might discuss having two pairs of shoes: one pair for weekdays and one for weekends?

Mma Ramotswe listened to all this without saying very much, other than punctuating Mma Makutsi's diatribe with a modest 'Very strange' and a cautious 'Rather unusual'.

'And she had the cheek to come in here and tell us,' Mma Makutsi fumed. 'The mother of the woman who . . .'

She left the accusation unfinished but Mma Ramotswe knew exactly what charge was envisaged. That was a sensitive issue, of course, but there was

177

a matter of principle here. The doors of the No. 1 Ladies' Detective Agency had always been open to whomsoever was in need. As Mma Makutsi well knew, they had sat and listened to the proud, the boastful, the arrogant, and even the moderately wicked. They had not condoned any of the human vices revealed to them, but they had always remembered that whatever the failings of the client, he or she was first and foremost a person in need of help. And there was still an element of doubt here. Sephotho was not a common name, but it was possible that this woman was nothing to do with Violet. They had not asked her, and she had offered no information that would have decided the matter one way or the other. Mma Ramotswe now raised this doubt, only to hear it being summarily swept aside by Mma Makutsi.

'Of course she is the mother,' she said. 'Look at her. And what was her name, Mma? Lily. Lily and Violet—two flowers. She must be the mother. If a flower has a child, what is that child? It is another flower, Mma, as in this case. Violet is the daughter of Lily.'

Mma Ramotswe had to acknowledge that if somebody was called Lily, then it was not unreasonable for her to call a daughter Violet, and so she did not argue. But she did point out—even if very mildly—that the sins of the father should not be visited upon the child, and by the same token the sins of the child should not be a pretext to berate the father.

'We are not talking about fathers and sons here, Mma,' said Mma Makutsi. 'We are talking about mothers and daughters.'

Mma Ramotswe looked at her watch. 'Well,

Mma, time is passing. It is already time for tea and we have so much work to do.'

'I will put the kettle on,' said Mma Makutsi briskly. 'We have had a very big shock this morning and tea will help us to get over it. That is what tea does. That is well known.'

Mma Ramotswe agreed that it was.

CHAPTER FOURTEEN

THE MIDFIELD STRIKER

After they had drunk their tea and the cups had been washed and stacked away, Mma Ramotswe and Mma Makutsi set about the tasks of the day. For both of them, the most pressing duty was to interview players from the Molofololo list. Mma Ramotswe was to see one of the new players, a young physical education teacher, while Mma Makutsi had an eleven o'clock appointment on the verandah of the President Hotel. Her player was a busy man, he warned her, a salesman, and he could spare only half an hour. He was prepared to speak to her, though, as long as she bought him coffee.

'That is very rude,' she complained to Mma Ramotswe. 'It is very ill-mannered to say that you will meet somebody but only if they buy you something.'

'Perhaps he was joking,' said Mma Ramotswe. 'There are people who talk like that, you know. They do not mean to be rude—they mean to be funny.'

'But I am not laughing,' said Mma Makutsi.

They left it at that, but when Mma Makutsi alighted from the minibus at the back of the President Hotel that morning she already felt that her meeting with Oteng Bolelang, an experienced attacking midfielder (whatever that was) in the Kalahari Swoopers, would be trying. The term *attacking midfielder* had been used by Mma Ramotswe when she had asked her assistant to speak to Bolelang, but Mma Makutsi was doubtful as to whether Mma Ramotswe knew what it meant. 'What is it?' she asked, and Mma Ramotswe had waved a hand and said, 'He attacks, Mma. He attacks from the middle of the field.' Mma Makutsi had considered this, but it was only later that she thought of the obvious retort. 'But what if the play has moved down to the other end of the field, Mma? What then? How can an attacking midfielder launch an attack when he is in the middle of the field and all the other players are down near the goalposts?' Mma Ramotswe would not have been able to answer that, she imagined, but then both of them were on very weak ground in this case and she was not one to talk. At least Mma Ramotswe had been to a football match, which was more than Mma Makutsi could claim.

The whole business, she thought as she made her way round the side of the President Hotel, was a complete waste of time. She and Mma Ramotswe would talk to these football players, with their ridiculous schoolboy-ish nicknames, and at the end of it all they would be none the wiser. Or they might be a little wiser in that they would have learned a bit more about the silliness of men's games, but they would not be wiser in their search for Mr Molofololo's traitor.

180

The square in front of the President Hotel, a large, well-used pedestrian thoroughfare known as the Mall, was more crowded than usual. The end-of-the-month pay-day had fallen a few days ago and the effect of the sudden injection of money into pockets was still being felt. All along the square, which ran from the government offices at one end to the bank offices at the other, small traders had set up their stalls. There were sellers of crudely made sandals, the shoes laid out before them in rows; dressmakers, with their racks of voluminous dresses; purveyors of traditional medicines, with their little piles of twisted roots and strips of bark; sellers of carvings and wooden salad bowls; hawkers of cheap sunglasses and perfumes. Business was being done—but not a great deal, as this spot seemed to provide for as many social as commercial opportunities. Questions were being asked about relatives and colleagues; marriages were being discussed and planned; complaints about the doings of officials and officialdom were being shared, and expanded; and, of course, news was being conveyed of distant cattle. There was a lot happening.

Mma Makutsi would have preferred to wander the length of the Mall, stopping to chat to people she recognised, but saw that she was already a few minutes late for her appointment. So, with the sinking heart of one obliged to perform an unwelcome task, she climbed up the open staircase that graced the front of the President Hotel and made her way on to the shaded verandah.

The hotel would become busy at lunch time, but now only a few of the tables were occupied. At one, a smartly dressed woman sat alone, a

181

magazine on the table in front of her. She was on edge, Mma Makutsi noticed, with the nervous look of one who is expecting to meet somebody important—somebody she was keen to impress, perhaps. From time to time she looked at a small mobile phone on the table; looked longingly, thought Mma Makutsi. Oh, my sister, Mma Makutsi said under her breath. Oh, my sister, I am sorry. He is not going to come, is he?

Mma Makutsi's gaze moved on. A middle-aged couple, visitors wearing large floppy hats, sat at a table poring over a tourist guide. Mma Makutsi smiled; so many people read these guides when they might have been looking around them and seeing the place they were reading about. It was the same with cameras: visitors spent so much time peering through the viewfinders of their cameras that they never looked at the country they were photographing. The couple lowered their books, though, and looked at her, smiled; her own smile grew wider. That was better. What does the book say about me? she wondered. *Look out for Mma Makutsi. She is the fiancée of Mr Phuti Radiphuti, and you should look out for him too.*

The brief reverie ended. There he was—there was no doubt about it—Mr Oteng Bolelang, midfield attacker, sitting at a table near the verandah parapet, pointedly looking at his watch.

'I am very sorry to be late, Rra,' she said, as she sat down at the table. 'But as Mma Ramotswe says, it is better to be late than to be *the* late.'

Oteng Bolelang looked at her in puzzlement. 'What is this? Who is this Mma Ramotswe?'

He spoke with an unusually high-pitched voice, which caught Mma Makutsi unawares. She had imagined that footballers—and especially midfield attackers—would speak with deep, masculine voices. This man, however, spoke with a rather thin, reed-like voice, the voice of a bird, she thought, or the voice of one of those thin dogs howling at the top of its register.

'Mma Ramotswe is the woman who owns the No. 1 Ladies' Detective Agency,' she said. 'That is who she is.'

Oteng gave a shrug. 'I do not know her.' His tone was peevish.

Mma Makutsi smiled pleasantly. 'Well, maybe one day you will meet her, Rra. She has asked me, though, to speak to you. You will know that Mr Molofololo wants you all to speak to us.'

'He told us that,' said the footballer. 'He thinks that we have nothing better to do than to talk to wo . . . talk to people.'

Women, thought Mma Makutsi. That is what you were about to say, but you stopped yourself. You do not like women, I think, Rra. You do not like us.

'I am sure that you are very busy, Rra,' she said. 'You told me on the telephone that you are a salesman. What do you sell?'

'Fridges,' said Oteng. 'Fridges and freezers.'

'That is very important in a hot country,' observed Mma Makutsi. 'Where would we be without fridges?'

'We would still be in Botswana,' said Oteng, looking again at his watch.

You are a very rude man, thought Mma Makutsi.

'Tell me, Rra. What is wrong with the team? Why is it always losing?'

183

Oteng looked at her as if he had been asked a completely unexpected question. 'That is a very strange question,' he said.

'Why is it strange?'

'Because it's so obvious that nobody should have to ask it.'

She waited for him to continue, but he did not, turning instead to catch the attention of the waiter who was hovering near the door. 'I need coffee,' he said.

Mma Makutsi was not going to let him derail her, and she repeated her question, adding, 'It may be obvious to you, Rra. But it is not obvious to me. The Swoopers used to win—now they lose. How would you explain that?'

'The goalie,' said Oteng. 'If the other side scores goals, then it is because the goalie lets them in. It is Big Man's fault.'

Mma Makutsi listened carefully. 'He's letting goals in?' she asked. 'He does that deliberately?'

Oteng burst out laughing—a superior, contemptuous laugh. 'No,' he said. 'It's much simpler than that. It's his eyesight.'

The waiter came to the table and Oteng ordered coffee. Almost as an afterthought, he asked Mma Makutsi whether she would like some too. *You are very, very rude*, she said to herself.

'What is wrong with his eyesight?' she asked.

'He needs glasses,' Oteng said. 'You can't have a goalie in glasses. It would look odd.'

Mma Makutsi thought for a moment. 'How do you know that he can't see very well? Has he told you?'

Oteng laughed again. 'Big Man Tafa doesn't speak to me much. He's jealous of me, of course.

184

I'm a midfield attacker, you know.'

Mma Makutsi nodded. 'I have heard that.'

'I saw him trip over something once,' he said. 'He didn't see it. I'm sure of it. And I threw him something once in the dressing room—just to test him. I threw him a pencil. I said, *Here, Big Man, catch this*. And he couldn't see it.'

'So that's the reason why the team isn't doing well?'

Oteng hesitated for a moment. 'Maybe.'

Mma Makutsi raised an eyebrow. 'There are other reasons, Rra?'

The high voice increased in volume, becoming shriller as it did so. 'Molofololo doesn't help. He keeps changing things. He changes tactics. He changes practice times. He changed all our kit when he got some new sponsor. We wanted to talk to him about that but he won't listen—the problem is that the sponsor pays for us to wear these things. He changed the club's telephone number and then changed it back again. You change things and everybody gets mixed up.'

The coffee arrived, and Oteng became taciturn. Mma Makutsi tried a few more questions but felt that she was getting nowhere. She too became silent. She did not offer to pour a second cup.

'You have been very helpful, Rra,' she said.

'Pleasure,' he said.

*   *   *

It was unusual for Mma Ramotswe to play any role in the running of the garage. She saw, though, Mr Polopetsi and the younger apprentice leaning against the side of a car; she saw that Fanwell was

185

drinking a cold drink out of a can and Mr Polopetsi was fiddling with what looked like a transistor radio—and she decided that Fanwell could be spared.

'You don't look very busy,' she said as she joined them. 'Are you fixing radios now, Rra?'

Mr Polopetsi laughed. 'This radio is almost finished,' he said. 'My wife said that we should throw it out but I am trying to save it.'

Mma Ramotswe looked at the apprentice. 'And you, Fanwell?'

'I have done all my work, Mma.' He gestured to the car behind him. 'This was much easier than we thought. All I had to do was . . .'

She did not need an explanation. Since things were so slack, she said, Mr Polopetsi could look after the garage and her office for a few hours, could he not? And Fanwell could come with her. 'You can drive my new van, Fanwell,' she said, dangling the keys in front of him. 'And you can help me with something.' She did not need to say what it was; a look sufficed.

Fanwell was particularly pleased to drive the van. 'This is very good, Mma,' he said as they pulled out into the traffic. 'Listen to that engine. It is like a bee. Bzz bzz. Like a very happy bee.'

Mma Ramotswe sighed. 'My old van made such interesting noises,' she said. 'Sometimes I thought that the engine was talking to me.'

Fanwell glanced at her. 'Yes, Mma. I think I understand how you feel.'

She returned his glance. A year ago she would never have imagined that either of the young men—Charlie or Fanwell—would understand such feelings. They liked speed and noise and loud music; they liked talking about girls and bars and football teams. Now it was different, and she realised how easy it is to misjudge the young, to imagine that they share none of the more complex emotions that shape our lives as we grow older. Well, they do, she said to herself; they have those feelings too, and suddenly they become capable of seeing them in others.

'Thank you, Fanwell,' she said. 'I miss that van. I miss it here.' She touched her chest, where her heart was.

He said nothing for a moment, but then half turned to face her.

Mma Ramotswe tapped his shoulder before he could say anything. 'You must watch the road while you're driving, Rra. Mr J. L. B. Matekoni says that most accidents happen when people are eating or trying to do something else while they drive.'

'I'm watching. I just wanted you to remember, Mma, what I said yesterday. I said that I couldn't guarantee anything. I might not be able to fix your van.'

She knew that, and reassured him that she did not expect a miracle. But as they approached Harry Moloso's scrapyard, she found her heart beating noticeably faster. It was only two days since the van had been towed away and she did not imagine that there was much that could have happened to it in that time. Yet it was possible. The van might already have been crushed in one of those machines that transformed a car body into a cube of compressed metal. That would be hard to bear—to see a tiny white cube where once there had been a living van.

'There's Harry Moloso's place,' said Fanwell,

187

pointing at an untidy-looking yard with a corrugated-tin fence. 'See it? It's a big place—it stretches all the way back there. Full of old cars, tractors, trucks—everything.'

They stopped at the gate, which was controlled by an elderly security guard in a khaki uniform. He came over and listened while Fanwell explained who they were and the nature of their errand. A barrier was raised—a gum-pole painted in red and white stripes—and they were in the yard.

'It is like the elephants' graveyard,' said Fanwell. 'You know that place where elephants go to die. All those white bones. Here it is the skeletons of cars.'

Fanwell was drawing up beside the office, a small breeze-block construction painted in lime green and with a large sign attached. *Harry Moloso, Mr Metal Magnet. Metal Resurrection-Miracles Daily.*

'He calls himself Mr Metal Magnet,' said Fanwell, pointing to the sign. 'That is a good name for a scrap merchant.'

Mma Ramotswe smiled weakly. She was gazing around the yard, looking for the tiny white van. At the back of the yard there were several old buses, wheel-less and listing heavily, their windows gaping holes; there were things behind them that she could not see from where she was standing. The tiny white van could easily be concealed there.

They walked up to the half-open door of the office.

'*Ko, ko!*' Mma Ramotswe called out.

A voice came from within. 'I'm in here. Come in, Mma.'

They pushed at the door, which moved back on

188

protesting hinges. For a rich man, as everybody said Harry Moloso was, he had not spent much money on his office. Here and there on the floor, some in small pools of oil, were engine parts, wrenched from old engines, wires and pipes, like discarded innards; elsewhere there were piles of papers, of trade directories and spare parts manuals, unfiled letters. It was like Mr J. L. B. Matekoni's office in the old days, before she and Mma Makutsi had jointly tackled it, but considerably worse than that.

'*Dumela*, Rra,' began Mma Ramotswe. 'You are Harry Moloso?'

The man sitting on a bench seat salvaged from an old car rose to his feet when they entered. He had been reading a newspaper, which he now folded and tossed down on a desk.

'I am Harry Moloso himself,' he said. He looked at Fanwell and winked. 'And you're the young man who works with Mr J. L. B. Matekoni, aren't you? You've been round for spares recently, I think.'

'I brought an old van round,' said Fanwell. 'I brought it along with Mr J. L. B. Matekoni.'

Harry Moloso nodded. 'Of course you did. A funny old white van. Ancient. Belonged to some fat lady, you said—suspension was shot on one side.'

Mma Ramotswe did not look at Fanwell. 'Traditionally built,' she whispered, just loud enough for the young man to hear.

Harry Moloso heard too. 'Yes, they built them very well in those days.'

Mma Ramotswe said nothing. Yes, they built vans *and* people well in those days.

'This lady is wanting to buy it back, Rra,' said

189

Fanwell.

Harry Moloso looked surprised. 'Back? It was yours was it, Mma?'

Mma Ramotswe nodded. 'It was my van, Rra. I'd like to try to have it fixed now. Fanwell here said that he could try.'

Harry Moloso looked at Fanwell. 'Quite a job, I'd say, Mr Big Mechanic.'

'Yes, Rra,' said Fanwell. 'But I'd like to try.'

Harry Moloso turned to Mma Ramotswe. 'I'm very sorry, Mma. You're too late. I sold that van almost immediately. Somebody came in.'

'Who bought it, Rra?' asked Fanwell quickly.

'No idea,' said Harry Moloso. 'Never seen him. He said that he came from Machaneng. He paid cash. Not very much, of course. He said he might try to fix it up.'

Mma Ramotswe hardly dared speak. 'And he . . . he . . .'

'Towed it away,' said Harry Moloso. He spoke gently, as if he realised that what he said was the end to a hope. 'He was taking it all the way up there. Four hours of towing, I'd say. Rather him than me.'

Fanwell thanked him, and they returned to the blue van. 'So,' the apprentice began, 'that looks like the end of the road for the white van, Mma. I'm very sorry.'

Mma Ramotswe looked out of the window, away from Fanwell, across the bleak field of broken metal. 'There is another road,' she said quietly. 'There is a road that leads to Machaneng.'

CHAPTER FIFTEEN

THERE ARE ALWAYS RED HERRINGS

Mma Ramotswe knew that she would worry about Mr J. L. B. Matekoni no matter how hard she tried not to. Concern for those whom one loved was an inescapable feature of this life—and it was impossible to imagine a world without such concern. But she did wish that he would not come home from Lobatse so late; that he would put his foot down and refuse to work beyond, say, five o'clock, which would mean that he would be back by half past six, well in time for his dinner, and she would not have to sit there and imagine what might have happened to him on the road home. Mr J. L. B. Matekoni would not change, though, and if a friend needed him to work late, then he would always do it.

When she got back to the office that day, she had not only paid a visit to Harry Moloso's scrapyard, but, having dropped Fanwell at the garage, she had gone on to interview one of the names on the list. This was the newest member of the team, the physical education teacher. The interview had left her none the wiser, and she was keen to hear what Mma Makutsi had discovered in her conversation with Oteng Bolelang. She felt that this investigation was not going to get anywhere, and she needed to talk to Mma Makutsi about it. Her assistant had expressed doubts—and perhaps these were better placed than she had imagined.

The solution to both the anxiety and the need to discuss the case was neatly provided by an invitation to dinner.

'I am going to be eating by myself this evening,' said Mma Ramotswe. 'The children are both staying with friends tonight—they like to do that, you know. They like to sleep over at their friends' houses. I think that they like to try different beds!'

'I remember that as a child,' Mma Makutsi said. 'I had a friend whose house was better than ours. I always liked going to sleep there. The food was better too.'

'Everybody else's food always is,' said Mma Ramotswe. 'Especially when you are a child. Everybody else always has a better life than your own. Their parents are nicer. Their house has more comfortable furniture. And so on.'

Mma Makutsi nodded. In her case, of course, everybody else's house really had been better, as the Makutsis did not have much money and this meant their home contained very little furniture. Now, of course, it was different; she had her salary and the money which Phuti gave her. And when she married—if that ever happened—then she would be even more comfortable. Perhaps Mma Ramotswe could come and sleep at her house then. They would have a large guest room with a big double bed and red curtains and . . .

'I wonder if you would like to eat with me tonight,' said Mma Ramotswe. 'I could make some nice stew, and we could talk. You could bring Phuti if you wanted.'

'He cannot come,' said Mma Makutsi quickly— rather too quickly? Mma Ramotswe asked herself—'but I would like that very much.' She was

pleased to receive this invitation from Mma
Ramotswe, as there was now no food at all left in
the house. Yesterday the choice had been between
shoes and groceries, and she had chosen shoes. As
a consequence Phuti had enjoyed a very frugal
meal—'Is there going to be a main course?' he had
asked at the end, and she had been obliged to
report that the kitchen cupboard was bare. 'I
almost bought more food,' she said, 'but . . .' The
but presaged a story of temptation and fall—a shoe
story, in fact—but Phuti had not pressed her and
the tale remained untold.

The two women agreed on a time and Mma
Ramotswe dropped in at the supermarket on the
way home to make sure that she had the necessary
supplies. She knew what Mma Makutsi's favourites
were, and she would make sure these were on the
menu. Mma Makutsi liked chicken, especially if it
was smothered in garlic, and she enjoyed ice
cream served with tinned South African pears.
Mma Ramotswe did not particularly like either of
these—certainly she avoided garlic and she found
that the slightly grainy texture of pears set her
teeth on edge. But she would provide both for
Mma Makutsi's sake.

Mma Makutsi arrived at the house early. She
had been invited for six o'clock, and arrived at ten
to six. 'It is always polite to arrive early,' she said. 'I
have read that ten minutes is about right.'

Mma Ramotswe looked doubtful. She read the
same magazines as did Mma Makutsi, and she was
sure that the advice she had seen was the direct
opposite of what Mma Makutsi had just claimed.
She would have to be careful, though, as Mma
Makutsi did not always welcome contradiction or

correction. In fact, she *never* welcomed either of these.

'I am not sure,' said Mma Ramotswe as she ushered her visitor into the kitchen. 'Are you certain that it's not, perhaps, a little bit the other way round? I'm not sure, of course, Mma. But why would they tell you to arrive early?'

'Because it's polite,' said Mma Makutsi. 'That is why, Mma. There are some things that are polite, and there are some things that are rude. It is polite to arrive ten minutes early.'

Mma Ramotswe pursed her lips. Mma Makutsi might be a person of firm views, and she might be somebody whom one would normally treat with great care, being slightly given to explosive reactions, but was it right to allow her to go through life believing something so clearly misguided as this? Mma Ramotswe thought not.

'Well, Mma, perhaps we should just think about it a bit.'

'No need,' said Mma Makutsi firmly, lowering herself on to a chair at the kitchen table. 'The rules of good behaviour are firm, Mma, as you well know. We know that it is wrong to take a present with one hand—we know that. It is just there, that rule, at least in Botswana. There may be countries where they have not heard of this—I know that—but I am not talking about such places. I am talking about Botswana. We cannot question these things.'

Mma Ramotswe took a pan down from the shelf. 'Yes,' she said. 'You are right, Mma, about these things. I would never say that you are wrong.'

'Good,' said Mma Makutsi.

'But at the same time,' Mma Ramotswe went on, 'it is possible to look at these rules and see what

194

lies behind them. That tells us why they exist. The reason for the rule against taking a present with one hand is that it looks as if you don't really appreciate the present—that you can only be bothered to use one hand to take it. That is why that one is there.'

Mma Makutsi was silent.

Mma Ramotswe took the opportunity to continue. 'And the rule about calling out *Ko, ko* before you go into a person's house is also there for a reason. If you do not call out in that way, then you may find the person who lives in the house without their clothes on or busy with something else. You never know what you will see in another person's house.'

Again Mma Makutsi said nothing. Emboldened, Mma Ramotswe moved on to the subject of arriving early. 'Now, if we think about the rule as to when you should arrive . . .'

Mma Makutsi broke her silence. She spoke loudly—and in a tone of authority. 'That rule says ten minutes early, Mma Ramotswe. That is what it says.'

'But let us look at that, Mma,' said Mma Ramotswe. 'Why should you arrive ten minutes early?'

'Because of the rule.'

'No. What is the *reason* behind the rule, Mma? If you arrive ten minutes early, then do you not think that it might be awkward for the person you're going to see? Not always, of course, but sometimes.'

'No,' said Mma Makutsi.

Mma Ramotswe tried again. 'You see, that person may not have finished cooking . . . She may have to look for a saucepan, or something like that. She may have to get things out of the fridge . . .' She made her way towards the fridge and took out the pieces of chicken she had set aside for their dinner.

Mma Makutsi looked unconvinced. 'I still think that it is better to be early, Mma. And that is why the rule is: always arrive ten minutes early.'

Mma Ramotswe decided that this was not an argument she could win. She would have to wait until the matter came up again in print—only then would it be possible to present Mma Makutsi with evidence capable of persuading her that she was wrong.

'Well, maybe there are two views on this,' Mma Ramotswe suggested mildly.

Mma Makutsi nodded vigorously. 'Yes. A right one and a wrong one, Mma.'

Mma Ramotswe turned away to hide a smile. She had to admire Mma Makutsi; so many people these days had no idea of what they believed and were quite happy to bend with whatever wind was blowing. Mma Makutsi was not like that.

She changed the subject. 'We need to talk about the Molofololo case,' she said. 'I have to get this chicken on the stove, but we can talk while I am cooking.'

'And I can help you,' offered Mma Makutsi.

Mma Ramotswe gave her assistant the task of peeling the potatoes while she relayed to her what she had learned at Big Man Tafa's house.

'So far,' she began, 'we know this: Big Man Tafa, the goalkeeper, wants to be captain. He thinks that Rops is past his best and should retire . . .'

'To the cattle post,' interjected Mma Makutsi.

'Yes, that is what his wife said. But there is more.'

Mma Makutsi, having peeled the first potato, held it up against the light. 'They must have talked a lot, Mma.'

Mma Ramotswe explained that she had also talked to an informant on the street. 'I learned that Big Man Tafa does not like Mr Molofololo. He said that he is always interfering. And then I learned that Big Man owes money. At least ten thousand pula.'

Mma Makutsi made her disapproval clear. 'Ten thousand pula! That is a lot, Mma. That gives him a very powerful motive, don't you think?'

Mma Ramotswe agreed, but pointed out that the person with the most obvious motive by no means always acts upon it. Motives, she reminded Mma Makutsi, could be what Clovis Andersen described as *red herrings*. She remembered the very passage, which she quoted to Mma Makutsi. *Always remember that life is never what we think it will be. There are always red herrings and their job is to mislead you. Never forget that!*

'So you don't think that it's Big Man Tafa?' asked Mma Makutsi.

Mma Ramotswe looked thoughtful. 'No, I do not think it's him, Mma. There are many reasons for it to be him, but I do not think it is.'

'Why not?'

'Because he doesn't *smell* guilty,' said Mma Ramotswe. 'You know how it is, Mma? Your nose tells you a lot of things. We must listen to our noses.' She was silent for a moment, again weighing Big Man in the balance. No, it was not him. 'No, Mma, Big Man is full of ambition, and he does not like Rops very much. But when I suggested to him that somebody was throwing matches away, I could tell that he was genuinely shocked. The nose, you see.'

Mma Makutsi found her eyes drawn inexorably to her employer's nose. It was not an exceptional nose in any way, and she wondered why it should have a greater ability than any other nose in this respect. But she thought that Mma Ramotswe was right; noses were useful and they did tell us a lot.

'And the teacher?' she asked. 'What did your nose say about him?'

Mma Ramotswe tapped the side of her nose. 'My nose was very clear on that one. The teacher is a very honest man.'

Mma Makutsi approved of this. 'Teachers should be honest. It is a great pity, Mma, that these days teachers are just like everybody else. I do not think that is right.'

Mma Ramotswe had views on that—she had great respect for teachers—but she did not want to get into a discussion of that just now. 'Not only was he honest,' said Mma Ramotswe, 'he was very fit. He took me to show me the new school gymnasium—a very fine room, Mma, with some ropes for children to swing on and a trampoline, Mma. He invited me to step on to the trampoline while we talked.'

Mma Makutsi shrieked. 'You didn't agree, did you, Mma?'

'I'm afraid that I did,' said Mma Ramotswe. 'I got on to it with him and he started to bounce. That made me start to bounce up and down too. We talked that way.'

Mma Makutsi said that she would have liked to

have seen that. 'I would not have laughed at you, Mma Ramotswe,' she said. 'But I would still have liked very much to see that. Did you find anything out about him?'

'Only that he is very keen,' said Mma Ramotswe. 'He likes everybody on the team—he had no bad words for anybody and he even praised Mr Molofololo. He said that he was very grateful to him for having given him a place on the team. And then he said that he was sure that the team would start to win again soon, especially since he was now on it. He said that he would make it his business to see that they won in future.'

'He's the one,' said Mma Makutsi. 'All the others have motives. He has none. He must be the one.'

'I wish it were that simple,' said Mma Ramotswe. 'And no, Mma, he is definitely not the one. My nose told me that. Again it was my nose.'

Mma Makutsi wondered what her own nose had told her about Oteng Bolelang. Her meeting with him had been a very unsatisfactory one, she told Mma Ramotswe, although she had learned that he suspected that Big Man Tafa could not see very well.

'What a strange thing,' Mma Ramotswe exclaimed. 'Did he actually say that, Mma?'

'Yes. He said that he had tested Big Man's sight by throwing him a pencil and Big Man had not caught it because he could not see well enough.'

Mma Ramotswe smiled. 'Or because he wasn't ready for it, don't you think, Mma? If I suddenly threw you something, would you be able to catch it?'

Mma Makutsi pondered this. Mma Ramotswe

was probably right. We did not expect people to throw things at us and therefore were not prepared. It was not surprising, then, if we failed to catch them.

'And there's another thing,' said Mma Ramotswe. 'People are always accusing players—and referees—of not being able to see. When I was at the Stadium, I heard people shouting out, *Where are your glasses, Ref?* I thought it very rude.'

'It is a very rude game altogether,' said Mma Makutsi.

'And did you learn anything else, Mma?'

Mma Makutsi told her about Oteng Bolelang's comments on Mr Molofololo. 'Apparently he is always changing everything. Outfits. Colours. Tactics. Even telephone numbers.'

Mma Ramotswe made a clucking sound. 'He is not popular with his players, you know, Mma. And you know what that means?'

Mma Makutsi peeled the last of the potatoes and dropped it into the saucepan of water that Mma Ramotswe had placed in the sink. 'What does it mean, Mma?'

'It means that all of them probably have a motive,' said Mma Ramotswe. She sounded discouraged. If every player had a motive, then how could they possibly single out the player who was responsible for the team's bad performance? And there was another possibility to consider: what if none of the players was responsible, and the reason for the decline of the team lay elsewhere? No, this was not going to be an easy case, and as she turned the chicken pieces in their oil, she wondered again whether this was not one of those cases that they would have been far wiser

200

to have refused. *Having a high success rate depends on the ability to say no to hopeless cases*, wrote Clovis Andersen. Once again, Clovis Andersen was right. He always was. Always.

They sat at the table and ate their chicken and potatoes. They had talked enough about the Molofololo case and were happy to speak about other things now. Mma Ramotswe was wary of raising the subject of Phuti and Violet Sephotho, but Mma Makutsi did that herself.

'I talked to Phuti when he came to eat last night,' she said.

Mma Ramotswe waited. 'And?'

'And I said to him: *How is Violet Sephotho doing in the shop?* And he said, *She is very good at her job—first class, in fact.* So I said, *Oh, I see. So she is a natural saleslady, is she?* And he said to me, *Yes, on the first day she sold four beds, and on the second she sold three. Then yesterday she sold two more. That is very good.*'

'It seems that there are many people needing new beds,' Mma Ramotswe observed.

'So it seems. And then I said to him: *Does she have far to travel to get to her work?* And he looked at me in a surprised way—you know how his nose wrinkles when he is puzzled?—and then he said, *No, she does not live too far away.* So I said, *Does she walk home then?* And he said, *That is a very strange question. Why are you so interested in this Violet person?*'

'Surely he can tell,' said Mma Ramotswe. 'Surely he can see what sort of woman she is?'

'Men are not very good at that, Mma,' Mma Makutsi said. 'We all know how they cannot tell these things. And so I said, *Did I not see her in your car?'*

Mma Ramotswe held her breath. 'And he said?'

Mma Makutsi popped a small piece of potato into her mouth. 'And he said, *Yes, I drove her home on that first day. She said that she had to be back in good time to cook a meal for her sick aunt.*' Mma Makutsi made her disbelief apparent.

'It is possible,' said Mma Ramotswe. 'I had an aunt who was not very well and . . .'

'Oh, anything is possible, Mma Ramotswe. It's just that I cannot imagine Violet cooking for a sick aunt. But I can imagine her telling Phuti a story like that so that he thinks, *This is a kind girl who is cooking for her aunt.* I can imagine that all right.'

The important thing, thought Mma Ramotswe, was how Phuti had reacted to Mma Makutsi's questioning. Did he sense that she was concerned about Violet?

'I don't think so,' said Mma Makutsi. 'But I am still very worried, Mma. What if she succeeds in making him fonder of her? What then? He is a good man, but even a good man can fall for a glamorous woman. That is well-known.'

'That is *very* well-known,' agreed Mma Ramotswe. 'Look at Adam. Look how he fell for Eve.'

'Just because she had no clothes on, he fell for her,' said Mma Makutsi.

'That sometimes helps,' said Mma Ramotswe.

They both laughed. And then it was time for pears and ice cream and the conversation shifted to talk about the first time that either of them remembered eating ice cream. 'I was eight,' said Mma Ramotswe. 'My father took me into Gaborone and he bought me an ice cream. I have never been so excited, Mma. It was a very great day for me.'

She closed her eyes. She was standing next to her father, the late Obed Ramotswe, that great man, and he was handing her an ice cream. He was wearing his hat, his battered old hat that he wore until the day he went into hospital for the last time. And he smiled at her from underneath the brim of that old hat, and the sun was behind him, high in the sky, and the ice cream tasted sweeter and purer than anything else she had ever tasted in her life. She would give anything—anything—to have her father back with her, just for a day, so that she could tell him about how her life had been and how she owed everything to him and to his goodness to her. It would not take long to tell him all that—about the same amount of time it takes to eat an ice cream or to walk the length of Zebra Drive. Not long.

Mma Ramotswe opened her eyes again, to see that Mma Makutsi was staring up at the ceiling. 'Why do you think we like ice cream so much, Mma?' Mma Makutsi asked. 'Or is that one of those questions that we can never answer?'

'I think it is,' said Mma Ramotswe, looking down at the table. There was one large helping of ice cream left—or two small ones. There was no doubt in her mind what was the right thing to do. 'You must have that ice cream,' she said, reaching across for Mma Makutsi's plate. She hoped that Mma Makutsi would say, 'No, we must share it, Mma.'

But Mma Makutsi did not. 'Thank you very much, Mma,' she said. 'You are very kind.'

She drove Mma Makutsi home in the blue van, dropping her off outside her lightless house. The evening was warm; night had brought little relief from the heat of the day, and the leaves of Mma Makutsi's two pawpaw trees, dark shapes against the moonlit sky, were drooping, as if with sheer exhaustion. The hot months were not easy— they drained the country of its energy, its vitality, crushing animals, people, plants under a sky that at times seemed like one great oven. And then, as the whole land became drier and drier and, in bad years, the cattle began to die, nature would relent, would remember that it was the time for rain. Great rain clouds, purple bank stacked upon purple bank, would appear above the horizon and then sweep in over the land with their longed-for gift of water. The temperatures would drop as the land breathed again; brown would become green; and the hearts of everything living would be filled with relief and gratitude. But that had not happened yet; it was still oppressively hot . . . and Mr J. L. B. Matekoni was still not back from Lobatse.

Mma Ramotswe looked at her watch as she drove away from Mma Makutsi's house. It was almost twenty to ten; their easy, woman-to-woman conversation had made the time pass quickly. Ten minutes to ten; if Mr J. L. B. Matekoni had finished work at eight o'clock—and surely it would have been unreasonable for them to keep him beyond that time—then he should have been back by nine fifteen. Of course he would have had to run Charlie home, and that could take, what?

Fifteen minutes, perhaps. There was not much traffic at this hour and none of those frustrating waits at traffic lights and intersections. If he had reached Game City at half past nine, allowing for a few minutes' delay at the police roadblock near the Mokolodi turn-off, then with fifteen minutes to get to Charlie's house and back . . . quarter to ten, then. But you always had to allow ten minutes or so leeway, so that meant that ten o'clock would be the latest she should expect him back. Now, if she took ten minutes to drive from Mma Makutsi's place back to Zebra Drive, then she should arrive back at the house at roughly the same time as he did.

She glanced in her rear-view mirror. Mma Makutsi had switched on a light, a single bulb outside her front door, and was waving. Goodnight, Mma: I am grateful to you. I am grateful to you for being my assistant and having all those peculiar ideas and insisting on them. I am grateful to you for being who you are: for standing up for ladies with large glasses and a bad skin and for everybody else who has had to battle to get where they have got. And most of all I am grateful to you for being my friend, Mma; I am grateful to you for that. That is the best thing that anybody can be to anybody else—a friend.

Her thoughts returned to Mr J. L. B. Matekoni. Somewhere in this country, somewhere in Botswana that day, somebody had been given news that would end their little world. Somebody, some unknown person somewhere, was being told that somebody else was not coming back. And all that stood between that poor person and oneself was chance, and luck, and forces that we would never

205

master nor understand. What if it was she who would be the recipient of such news this night? No, she could not think about that, she would not. But it could happen, couldn't it?

She turned into Zebra Drive. Her hands were shaking now, and inside her, in that strange, indefinable region where the physical side of dread makes its presence known, she felt a sense of dreadful imminence, a rawness.

Her gate appeared before her, and beyond that, in the beam of the headlights, the four small pillars of her verandah. She swung the van round to negotiate the turn into the short drive and as the beam of the lights moved round she saw the back of the truck, the lights still glowing red. The other vehicle's lights went off, but it was now illuminated in her headlights, and she saw Mr J. L. B. Matekoni step out and dust off his trousers, as he always did when he alighted from his truck. And she stopped her van where it was, some yards short of its normal place at the side of the house, and she got out and ran to him, the lights of the van still burning—to show the world, if anybody was walking in that darkness along Zebra Drive, if anybody cared to look, the reunion, after one day away, of a man and his wife, of Mr J. L. B. Matekoni, returned safely from Lobatse, the finest mechanic in Botswana, and Mma Ramotswe, his wife, who loved him more dearly than she had ever loved anybody else before, with the possible exception of Obed Ramotswe, her father, retired miner, fine judge of cattle, now late.

CHAPTER SIXTEEN

CHARLIE LOOKS AT BEDS

Big Man Tafa's wife, Mmakeletso, had said that her husband had said—so much of what Mma Ramotswe was picking up was second-hand information, *hearsay* as Clovis Andersen would put it—that Mr Molofololo was, amongst other things, impatient. Well, he is, thought Mma Ramotswe, as she listened to him on the telephone the next morning.

'Have you found this man, Mma Ramotswe? You have had quite a few days now. Which one is it?'

Mma Ramotswe raised an eyebrow, silently mouthing the liquid syllables of his name to let Mma Makutsi know who was on the other end of the line: *Molofololo.*

'We have been making good progress, Rra,' she assured him. 'My assistant and I are actively interviewing the players on that list you gave us. We are uncovering a considerable amount of information. Many interesting things.'

'Such as?' Mr Molofololo snapped.

Mma Ramotswe hesitated. She could hardly tell him—at this stage at least—that some of the players, possibly most of them, found him an irritation. Nor did she want to tell him that Big Man Tafa was in debt and that he wanted Rops out of the way, or that Oteng Bolelang was arrogant and considered Big Man Tafa to be in need of glasses. So she simply said, 'Many interesting things, Rra, that I shall be using to build up a picture of what's going on.'

'But I know what's going on,' said Mr Molofololo. 'What's going on is that one of my players is throwing the matches. We have a traitor, Mma, and that is why I'm paying you good money to find out who it is.'

Mma Ramotswe thought that she might point out that he had paid nothing so far. She had asked for a small sum on account but her request had been ignored.

'I think we should meet soon, Rra,' she said. 'Then we can have a good talk about the case. It's not easy to talk about these things on the telephone.'

Mr Molofololo was quick to accept the offer. 'You could come to the match on Saturday,' he said. 'We're playing the Molepolole Squibs. Come to that and we can talk then.'

Mma Ramotswe thought of her weekend. She had already sacrificed one precious Saturday afternoon to sit watching an unintelligible set of events unfolding on the pitch, and she did not see any point in doing that again. Puso, on the other hand, would very much see the point.

'I think that it is best to talk somewhere else,' she said. 'There is always too much going on at a football match and . . . and I must be discreet, you know.'

'Ah yes,' said Mr Molofololo. This was how he imagined detectives operated—discreetly. 'You're right, Mma. Keep a low profile. But what about Puso—that is his name, isn't it? He is a good little boy—would he like to come to the match?'

'He would like that very much, Rra. You are

very kind.'

'And then we can talk on Monday?'

'On Monday, Rra. And by then, I hope, I shall have something for you.'

She regretted that remark the moment she had made it. It was a bad mistake to tie yourself down to deadlines—it was a bad mistake to make promises in general—but there was something about Mr Molofololo's manner—his pushy, rather hectoring style—that led to this. Was this what the players objected to, she wondered, and could it have triggered sufficient resentment in some breast to motivate treachery?

She replaced the receiver after her conversation with Mr Molofololo and exchanged glances with Mma Makutsi.

'More interviews, I'm afraid, Mma,' she said.

Mma Makutsi shrugged. 'We will know a lot about football at the end of it all, Mma. We will be able to talk to men about it.'

Mma Ramotswe chuckled. 'I believe that there are some ladies who learn about football in order to do just that. They know that that is what men like to talk about. It helps them find men.'

'Violet Sephotho,' said Mma Makutsi.

Mma Ramotswe kept a tactful silence.

'Yes, Violet Sephotho is the sort who would do that,' Mma Makutsi went on. 'Football, furniture— she'll do anything to get her hands on a man.'

'Are you still worried?' asked Mma Ramotswe.

'Of course I'm worried, Mma. Phuti is a good man, and I trust him. But even a good man can sometimes be . . . not so good.'

Mma Ramotswe had to agree. She had come across so many different types of people in her job,

209

and she knew that even those who were strong could find times when they were weak. It was not really their fault, because we were all human and being human made us weak. But it happened.

'Have you heard anything else?'

Mma Makutsi did not reply immediately and Mma Ramotswe knew from her silence that there had been something else.

'I have heard something,' Mma Makutsi said eventually. 'I met one of the ladies who works in Phuti's shop. It was in the supermarket. She told me that over the last few days, Violet has sold even more beds. Apparently Phuti is so pleased that he has been talkling about promoting her to . . .' She paused. It clearly cost some effort just to say it. 'Assistant manager.'

Mma Ramotswe was shocked. 'Of the whole store?'

Mma Makutsi shook her head. 'No, not the whole store. But of that floor. Assistant floor manager.'

Mma Ramotswe whistled. 'That is very bad, Mma. But how has she been selling all these beds? Is she really such a great saleslady?'

'It is a mystery,' said Mma Makutsi. 'Maybe she is persuasive. I don't know. But one thing she did tell me, Mma—that other woman—she said that all the customers, except for one, were men.'

Mma Ramotswe had been sitting back in her chair during this conversation; now she sat bolt upright.

'Men, Mma?'

'Men.'

Mma Ramotswe rose to her feet. She did not go anywhere—she simply rose to her feet, and Mma

Makutsi knew this for the signal that it was. Mma Ramotswe had experienced a moment of insight.

'Mma Makutsi,' she said, her voice quiet, but tense with excitement. 'Please go and see if Charlie is free. Even if he isn't free, ask him to come in here and talk to me.'

Mma Makutsi headed for the door. 'What do you want to ask him to do, Mma?'

'He needs to buy a bed,' said Mma Ramotswe.

*   *   *

Charlie came in beaming. There had been an increasing jauntiness about him recently, noticed by both Mma Ramotswe and Mma Makutsi, but commented upon by only one of them. 'He's up to something, Mma,' said Mma Makutsi. 'See the way he's walking? See the way his legs go up and down like that?'

'But everybody's legs go up and down,' Mma Ramotswe pointed out mildly.

It was as if Mma Makutsi had not heard. 'And his bottom, Mma. I do not wish to be indelicate, but see how his bottom sticks out.'

'Everybody's bottom sticks out,' said Mma Ramotswe. 'That is normal, Mma.' She paused. There were exceptions, of course. Those thin, modern people who spent all their energy on reducing the size of their clothing—they must have a most uncomfortable time of it sitting down, with very little padding.

And now here was Charlie sauntering into the office, wiping his hands on one of the pieces of lint that Mr J. L. B. Matekoni insisted on using, in spite of the ubiquity of paper towels.

'What is it, Mma Ramotswe?' he asked. 'Are you ladies having difficulty adding figures or something like that? I'm your man for that. Best in class for mathematics at the Botswana Automotive Trades College—two years running. One, two, three, four—I'm your man.'

'Excuse me,' said Mma Makutsi as she made her way back to her desk. 'If you were best in class at that college of yours, then why have you not finished your apprenticeship? Answer that, Mr Charlie.'

Charlie did not look at Mma Makutsi, but addressed Mma Ramotswe in the tone of one unjustly attacked. 'You hear that, Mma Ramotswe? You hear what that lady over there has said? Not everyone finishes their apprenticeship in double-quick time. It is sometimes better to do things thoroughly. You should not rush.'

'Of course, Charlie,' said Mma Ramotswe soothingly. 'You finish your apprenticeship in your own time. It does not matter. Some people never even do an apprenticeship.'

She had not intended this to be a jibe, but Charlie seized on it immediately. Spinning round, he pointed triumphantly at Mma Makutsi. 'Some detectives, for example, Mma! Some people who call themselves assistant detectives never did a detective apprenticeship in their lives! Ha!'

'Hush, Charlie,' said Mma Ramotswe. 'We do not want to have an argument in here. This office is a peaceful place. This is Botswana, remember.'

'She . . .'

Mma Ramotswe cut him short. 'Now, look, Charlie, we have a very important job for you. This is something that requires a very good actor.

Somebody who could be in films . . .'

'If he finished his apprenticeship,' chipped in Mma Makutsi.

Mma Ramotswe threw a discouraging glance at her assistant. 'Please! Please! Thank you! Now what we want you to do, Charlie, is to come with us—with Mma Makutsi and me. We are going to the Double Comfort Furniture Shop—you know, that's the place that belongs to Mr Phuti Radiphuti.'

'Old Phuti,' said Charlie.

'And once we get there,' Mma Ramotswe persisted, 'we would like you to go in and pretend that you are interested in buying a bed. Go to the bed department and you will find a lady there called Violet . . .'

'Violet Sephotho!' exclaimed Charlie. 'The one we chased in the supermarket. The one with the bottom like that.' He made an expansive gesture.

Mma Ramotswe shook her head. 'You should not talk like that, Charlie. But yes, she is a very glamorous lady.'

'Oh, is that what husband-stealers are called these days?' interjected Mma Makutsi. 'That is a very good name for such a lady, I think.'

Mma Ramotswe allowed this to pass. 'Yes, she is a glamorous lady, Charlie. And all I want you to do is to pretend that you are very interested in buying a bed. Say that you have just moved here from Francistown. Say that you had a very good job there with one of the mining companies and now you are going to be based in Gaborone, and need a new bed. Tell her that you would like a double bed—that you are not married or anything like that, but that you would like a good-sized bed.

That is all you have to say.'

Charlie clapped his hands together enthusiastically. 'I am a very good actor, Mma. This will be no problem.'

'I'm sure you're a good actor, Charlie. I'm sure you'll do it very well. But one thing: could you pretend that you're not too sure about the bed she tries to sell you. Say that you will have to think about it and that you may need to look at beds in some other shops. Pretend to be one of those customers who always need persuading.'

'And then?'

'And then, after you have said all this, and she has said all that she says, you can say that you have to go, but that you will be back later. Don't sign anything, whatever you do.'

'I never sign things, Mma,' said Charlie. 'If you give people your name, then they get you. I have always known that. *Watch out* is my motto!'

Mma Makutsi thought this very amusing. 'Good one, Charlie. Watch out, here comes Charlie. Good motto, Charlie.'

Mma Ramotswe allowed herself a small smile at this, as did Charlie. This banter between Mma Makutsi and Charlie was not all that serious, she thought. In fact, she believed that underneath it all they probably liked each other, difficult though it was at times to see this affection in action. People have strange dealings with one another, Mma Ramotswe felt: those who appear on the surface to be friends may in reality be enemies—but how could you tell? And did it happen the other way round? Take Mr Molofololo: he had many enemies, it seemed, or at least many people who appeared not to like him for some reason or other.

But how many of these enemies were really friends? It was easy to imagine why an enemy might wish to appear a friend, but why, she wondered, would a friend claim to be an enemy?

Mma Makutsi now raised an objection. 'One thing about this plan, Mma: what if she recognises Charlie from that time in the supermarket?'

Mma Ramotswe had thought of that and discounted the possibility. The encounter in the supermarket had been fraught, but it had mainly involved her and Mma Makutsi. Charlie had been in the background and had said nothing, which meant that in the heat of the altercation Violet probably barely noticed him.

'She won't recognise him,' she said. 'And, anyway, even if she does, it won't matter. Even young men who work in garages need beds, don't they?'

'We all need a bed,' mused Mma Makutsi. 'Everybody needs a bed.'

Mma Ramotswe nodded. 'That is certainly well known,' she said.

Mma Makutsi looked thoughtful. 'One other thing, Mma. Why are you asking Charlie to do this? What do you hope to prove?'

'We'll see,' Mma Ramotswe replied. 'Sometimes you don't know what you're looking for until you find it. Would you not agree, Mma?'

'I'm not sure, Mma. I would have to think about it.'

'Well, it's true,' said Mma Ramotswe. 'It really is.'

*   *   *

They parked the blue van outside the Double Comfort Furniture Shop, and while Charlie made his way inside Mma Ramotswe and Mma Makutsi sat in the cab of the van, the windows down for the heat. Fortunately they had found some shade under one of those handy acacia trees that in the hot weather were to cars like honeycombs to bees. This one already had several vehicles nudged under its shade but there was just enough room for the blue van.

After ten minutes, Mma Makutsi began to get anxious. 'What is he doing in there, Mma? Do you think that he'll be trying out all sorts of chairs and things? Phuti says that some people come in just to sit in his comfortable chairs. He says that they often have no intention of buying anything. Sometimes he finds people asleep in the big armchairs and he has to wake them up.'

In bringing up the subject of chairs, she reminded herself of Phuti's promise to give her a new one for the office. She had not raised the matter again, and now was unsure what to do about it. The problem was that she felt that she could not have a new chair while her boss, Mma Ramotswe, still had an old one. And yet if she declined Phuti's offer, then he would surely be offended . . . It was all very difficult.

Mma Ramotswe meanwhile had been envisaging Phuti's customers sitting in those comfortable armchairs. 'We all need to sit down,' she said.

'Yes, but not in chairs that don't belong to us,' countered Mma Makutsi. 'That's the trouble with this country, Mma—there are too many people sitting down in other people's chairs.'

It was another of Mma Makutsi's odd statements—utterly unfounded in fact, Mma Ramotswe suspected, but not a point that she wished to argue. As far as she was concerned, if a chair was empty, then anybody should be welcome to sit in it. We should share our chairs, she felt. Maybe that was the real problem with the modern world—not enough of us were prepared to share our chairs. Yes, that was probably true, and she wondered whether she might not have a word with Bishop Mwamba and suggest that he talk about that in a future sermon. He could start off, perhaps, by asking the members of the congregation whether they had noticed how many chairs there were and how many of them were empty. That would get them thinking. But where would it go from there? That would be up to Bishop Mwamba, she decided: he was good at sermons and he would surely find some way of deriving an important lesson from chairs.

This line of thought led to Professor Tlou. Mma Ramotswe was a great admirer of Professor Tlou and she had read somewhere a reference to the fact that he had a chair of history. She knew that this was just a way of talking—that it simply meant that he was a professor of the history of Botswana—but she thought that it would be rather nice if the university were to give him an actual chair to go with the title. The chair of history, she felt, would have to be a very old chair, one of those chairs made out of dark hardwood with carved legs and an elaborate criss-cross seat of tightened animal-hide strips. It would be a very venerable chair, that chair, and quite unlike a chair of music, which would issue little musical squeaks when you sat in it, or which would make a sweet singing sound if it were left outside and the wind blew through it.

Her thoughts were interrupted by a nudge from Mma Makutsi.

'He's coming, Mma,' she hissed. 'Look.'

Charlie walked jauntily out of the front door of the shop and made directly for the van. There was no room for him in the cab—he had travelled in the open section at the back—but they needed to talk to him now and so they both got out to greet him and led him to a shady place under the acacia.

'Well?' asked Mma Ramotswe.

Charlie rolled his eyes heavenwards. 'She's quite a lady, that one! One, two, three!'

'Never mind all that, Charlie,' said Mma Makutsi impatiently. 'What happened?'

'Give him time, Mma,' said Mma Ramotswe. 'Tell us, Charlie, but take your time about it. Try to remember everything, please.'

Charlie enjoyed being the centre of attraction. 'Well now,' he began. 'I went into the store. That's quite a store, Mma Ramotswe! No wonder Mma Makutsi is happy to be engaged to that Phuti! Big store, Mma. Big store.'

Mma Ramotswe coaxed him on. 'Yes, yes, Charlie. But what about the bed?'

Charlie smiled. 'I found that lady you were talking about—that Violet lady. My, my! Pretty lady that one. Pretty lady! Anyway she comes up to me—like this, this is how she walks, see—and she says, *You're looking for a bed, Rra? Yes? This is the right place. You've come to the best place in Botswana for beds.* And so on.'

'And then?'

218

'And then she says, *This bed here, Rra, is a very good bed for you, I think. Try it.* She said that I should lie down on the bed and see whether it was comfortable. So I did that. And while I was lying down, she comes up beside me and says, *You look very handsome there, Rra, lying on that bed—very handsome.* So I sit up and she says, *What do you think of that bed, Rra—isn't it the most comfortable bed you've ever tried?* And then she says, *I'm sure a handsome young man like you, Rra, has slept in many beds!* And she laughed.'

Mma Ramotswe and Mma Makutsi exchanged disapproving glances.

'And then, Charlie?' pressed Mma Ramotswe. 'And then what happened?'

'Then I got up and poked at the mattress with my finger and felt the wooden headboard. Very smooth. And I said, *Well, I'm not too sure, really, about this bed. I will need to look at beds in other shops. It's a big purchase, you know.* And then . . .' He paused, adding extra dramatic effect to what he was about to say. 'And then, Violet came up and whispered to me, *If you buy this bed, Rra, then one day soon I'll come along and help you try it out.* That is what she said! Some lady, Mma Ramotswe! Ow! Onc, two, three!'

Mma Ramotswe's eyes opened wide. 'I knew it!' she exclaimed. 'I knew it, Mma Makutsi! That is how Violet Sephotho manages to sell so many beds.'

Mma Makutsi shook her head. 'It is so shameful,' she said. 'It is so shameful that this has been happening under Phuti's nose and he did not know what she has been saying to the customers.'

Charlie raised a finger. 'Maybe he does, Mma.'

Mma Makutsi frowned. 'What do you mean, Charlie?'

Charlie looked awkward. 'I might have told him myself, Mma. I didn't mean to, but . . . Well, you see, what happened was this. After I had told her that I was going to think about it, I started to leave. But I saw a man looking at one of the beds as if he was inspecting it. As I walked past him I whispered, *You should buy one of these beds, Rra! You get a lot of extras!* I was just trying to be friendly—one man talking to another, you know. Anyway, he stood up, this man and he turned round and I saw it was your Phuti Radiphuti, Mma Makutsi. Yes! And he said, *What are you talking about?* So I told him and he started to shake—like this, Mma—and he said, *She is a very wicked lady* and he walked off towards her and I came out, Mma. That is all.'

Mma Ramotswe looked at Mma Makutsi. 'I do not think that we need to do anything more, Mma,' she said. 'Phuti now knows about the . . .'

'Bad woman in his bed,' supplied Mma Makutsi, adding, quickly, 'department.'

CHAPTER SEVENTEEN

TEA WITH MMA POTOKWANI

Over the next few days the staff of the No. 1 Ladies' Detective Agency—that is Mma Ramotswe and Mma Makutsi, with some assistance from Mr Polopetsi—were more than usually busy. The atmosphere in the office, though, was not as strained as it sometimes was during busy periods; in fact, it was rather light-hearted, not dissimilar to the mood that prevailed in the weeks before Christmas, when everybody was looking forward to parties and celebrations. Christmas was, of course, still some time away; what led to the lightness of mood now was the evident happiness of Mma Makutsi. The tensions that had arisen on the appointment of Violet had disappeared the very afternoon of Mma Ramotswe's exposure of the real reason for her sales success. Phuti Radiphuti, an upright man, had been profoundly shocked to hear of her sales technique, and had dismissed Violet immediately. The enraged former manager of the bed department had stormed out, meeting Mma Ramotswe and the others, still standing beside the van in the car park.

'It is you, Mma Ramotswe, who has done this thing to me,' she hissed. 'I shall not forget it.' And then, seeing Mma Makutsi waiting in the van, she had shaken a finger at her erstwhile classmate and shouted abuse in her direction. 'And you, Grace Makutsi! Don't you think that I don't know that you've been involved in this. Well, if I were you, I'd hang on to your precious Phuti Radiphuti very tight. He really likes me, you know. He couldn't keep his hands off me, you know. And he an engaged man!'

'Don't believe her,' called out Mma Ramotswe as she approached the van. 'Phuti would never.'

'Oh yes he would,' yelled Violet. 'And he did.'

Mma Ramotswe was now at the van and she climbed into the cab, emphasising to Mma Makutsi the meretricious nature of everything that Violet said. 'Do not believe that woman,' she said. 'She is jealous of you. And Phuti is a good, upright man. He is still your fiancé—that is what Violet cannot stand.'

'I trust Phuti,' said Mma Makutsi. 'He would never go near a woman like her. And I never thought he would.'

This, thought Mma Ramotswe, was not strictly true—Mma Makutsi had been convinced that Violet presented a very real danger—but she did not argue. The important thing was that Mma Makutsi's mood was back to normal and that they would be able to get on with their work on the Molofololo case in reasonably good spirits. Not that Mma Ramotswe dared hope that they were getting anywhere with that inquiry—indeed, it was remarkable how similar were the responses of all the other players they had spoken to that week.

Even Rops Thobega, who was interviewed by Mma Ramotswe and Mma Makutsi together, had much the same view as Big Man Tafa and the others about the interference of Mr Molofololo. 'He means well,' said Rops, 'but I wish he would stop meaning quite so well. He's always changing things, you know. Do things this way—no, do them this way. All the time. And then six months ago he went and changed all our kit—shorts, strips, socks, boots, the lot. He had some new sponsor who got him all this kit and he made us use it. It's never-ending. Change, change, change. Nag, nag, nag. And he never listens to us. Never.'

She had wondered about Big Man, and about one or two of the others, but had decided, in the end, that there really was nobody at whom the finger could be pointed. Nor a nose either.

At the end of the week, Mma Ramotswe began

222

to draft the report that she planned to submit to Mr Molofololo the following Monday. She dictated it to Mma Makutsi, sitting in their office, in the heat of mid-morning, watching the flies on the ceiling as she spoke.

'My assistant and I have jointly spoken to every member of the team. We have found no notable instances of disloyalty. Every member appears to be fond of the Kalahari Swoopers and we found no evidence that any one of them would willingly do anything to ensure that opposing teams won. At the same time we found that there was . . .'

She paused. 'How should I put that, Mma?' she asked Mma Makutsi.

'We found that there was some *dissatisfaction*,' suggested Mma Makutsi.

'Very good. We found that there was some dissatisfaction with the style that you yourself adopt in telling the team what to do. We do not wish to give offence, Rra, but we must tell you that the team might play better if you did not spend so much time changing tactics and telling them what to do. In conclusion, therefore . . .'

Again Mma Makutsi provided the form of words. 'You should say, *In conclusion, we think that there is no evidence of a traitor and all inquiries of this nature should be terminated—after payment of our bill, which we now append to this report as appendix 1(a).*'

'That is very good,' said Mma Ramotswe. 'You are very good with words, Mma. And I am happy enough with this report now, even though it says really very little . . .'

'It says nothing,' said Mma Makutsi, closing her notebook with a flourish. 'But that, Mma, is because there are some cases in which there is nothing to say.'

*   *   *

When Saturday came, Mma Ramotswe arranged for Mr J. L. B. Matekoni to drop Puso off at the football ground where the Kalahari Swoopers were due to play the Molepolole Squibs. Mr J. L. B. Matekoni had toyed with the idea of going too, but had decided, in the end, to catch up on his accounts, which he had sorely neglected over the last month. If you send bills, Mma Ramotswe had pointed out to him, then people forget to pay you. He knew that was true, and yet there always seemed so many other things to do—more important things, he felt, such as finding what was wrong with a particularly cantankerous car, or looking for a spare part for Mma Potokwani's old van, or any of the other things that a generous-hearted mechanic finds himself asked to do. Of course it would have been simpler had he insisted on payment in every case before a vehicle was removed—every other garage did that—but how could he turn a car in need away simply because of its owner's temporary impecuniosity? He could not, and Mma Ramotswe—and everybody else, particularly impecunious drivers—loved him for it.

So it was accounts, rather than football, for Mr J. L. B. Matekoni, and for Mma Ramotswe it was, to her immense satisfaction, a perfectly ordinary Saturday. She would do her shopping with Motholeli before dropping her off to play at a friend's house. Then she would have tea at the President Hotel, perhaps call in on a friend for a further cup of tea, walk in her garden, sit on her verandah, plan the evening meal, and have an afternoon nap on her bed with the latest copy of her favourite magazine. That would be the best part of it all—lying on the bed reading helpful household hints and about the exotic, patently doomed romance of some distant person, before allowing the magazine to slip out of her hand as sleep—dreamless afternoon sleep—overtook her.

Puso, of course, was bursting with excitement as he prepared for his football outing. This excitement was mixed with a certain self-importance: he had been told to report to Mr Molofololo when he arrived at the game, and he would be allowed to help the team get ready. He now spoke of the team as 'us' and Mr Molofololo as 'my friend, Rra Molofololo'. But he was realistic, too, for all his enthusiasm, and told Mr J. L. B. Matekoni as they drove to the match that he thought it likely that the Molepolole Squibs would win.

'You never know,' said Mr J. L. B. Matekoni. 'You never know what can happen.'

'We will not play well,' said Puso. 'We are full of bad luck at the moment.'

And when he was collected at the end of the match, his expression told Mr J. L. B. Matekoni everything, even before the young boy had climbed into the cab of the truck.

'No?' asked Mr J. L. B. Matekoni.

'The Squibs won,' said Puso. 'They are not a very strong team but they won. They scored so many goals.'

'But it was a good game?' asked Mr J. L. B. Matekoni.

225

'If you were a Squib,' said Puso.

Mr J. L. B. Matekoni was thoughtful. There would have to be a lesson about sportsmanship, and about enjoying a game, no matter what the outcome. It was sometimes a hard lesson to be learned, and some people never learned it, but it was needed. He looked at Puso, and tried to remember what it was like to be that age. You wanted things so much—that was it: you wanted things so much that you *ached*. And sometimes you believed that you could make the things you yearned for happen, just by willing them. He had done that himself—he remembered it vividly, when as a boy he had lost a favourite uncle and he had walked out into the bush and looked up at the sky and addressed God directly: *Please make him not be dead. Please make him not be dead.* And when he had got home, he had half expected that his act of willing would have somehow worked and his uncle would have miraculously recovered. But of course there was still the sound of keening women and the black armbands and all the other signs that it had not worked: the world is the world in spite of all our wishes to the contrary.

When they returned to the house, Mma Ramotswe was up from her nap and was chopping onions in the kitchen. Mr J. L. B. Matekoni told her that the Kalahari Swoopers had not played well—as everyone expected—and that Puso was taking it badly.

'He'll learn,' she said. 'We all learn about losing.'

'Except Mr Molofololo,' mused Mr J. L. B. Matekoni. 'I'm not sure that he's learned about losing.'

'No,' said Mma Ramotswe. 'Some people like that seem not to have learned these simple lessons.'

Puso came into the kitchen and began to tell her about the game. After a few minutes, she lost track of what he was saying. It was something about tackles and fouls and penalties—technical details that she had heard people talking about over the past weeks but that still meant very little to her. And then, by chance, she said, 'And did you talk to the players? Did Mr Molofololo let you help, as he said he would?'

Puso nodded. 'I was allowed to hold the ball while they were waiting to go on. Some of them talked to me.'

She began to peel another onion. She was not really interested in football any more, now that she had written her report and was intending to bring the investigation to an unsatisfactory conclusion. But Puso was, and she was listening with half an ear. 'And what did they say?' she asked.

'Most of them said they didn't like their boots,' he said. 'One of them said that they were very uncomfortable, and the others all joined in.'

Mma Ramotswe hesitated. She put down the onion.

'They said that their boots were uncomfortable?'

'Yes. They said that Mr Molofololo had made them wear boots that a sponsor had given them. They said that they had been wearing them for six months and they were still uncomfortable. I thought they looked very nice . . .'

Mma Ramotswe looked out of the window. It was so obvious. So obvious. But then the solutions

227

to complex problems were often such simple things. If you wore uncomfortable boots, then how could you play good football? Of course you cannot—everybody, even a woman who owned a detective agency and who came from Mochudi and who had a fine mechanic for a husband, and two children who loved her although she was not their real mother, and who was the daughter of a man called Obed Ramotswe—even such a woman, with absolutely no knowledge of football, and no interest in it—even she would know that.

Then she remembered something, and the remembering of it struck her so forcefully that she found herself holding her breath, almost afraid to breathe. Of course. Of course. Mr Molofololo had made that strange remark, right at the beginning: *I am the one. It is me.* He knew! He knew—on one level—that he was the problem, and it had slipped out. He knew but did not know, as was often the case with a person's own faults. We know what is wrong but we cannot bring ourselves to admit it. She had helped clients like that before—people who really knew the answer to their problems but wanted somebody else to help them admit it. She breathed out. Yes. Yes.

She turned round and suddenly picked Puso up and hugged him. It was exactly the sort of gesture that a small boy would find acutely embarrassing— that they would run away from to avoid—but he suffered it. 'You clever, clever boy!'

The boy's embarrassment turned to puzzlement. 'Why, Mma?'

'Oh, Puso, it is a very big case that you have just solved. What . . . what treat would you like? Tell me.'

He looked up at her. 'Ice cream,' he said. 'Lots of it.'

'There will be ice cream,' she said. 'We shall go right now. In the van. Ice cream—lots and lots of ice cream. More than you can eat—I promise you.'

*　　　*　　　*

The following Monday morning, at eleven o'clock, Mma Ramotswe drove out to the orphan farm to have tea with Mma Potokwani. She had received no specific invitation, and when she left the office of the No. 1 Ladies' Detective Agency she had no idea even that the matron would be in. But in the event she received her usual warm greeting from her friend, who was standing in front of her office in an apparently idle moment.

'Nothing to do, Mma Ramotswe?' Mma Potokwani called out. 'Time for a cup of tea?'

'You do not look very busy yourself,' replied Mma Ramotswe, as she walked up to greet her.

'I am standing here planning,' said Mma Potokwani. 'I do my best thinking when I am on my feet watching the children playing.'

Mma Ramotswe looked round. A group of very small children were playing under a tree—some strange game of childhood that involved tagging and running. There had been so many of those games, thought Mma Ramotswe—all with complicated rules and a history behind them; just like the affairs of the adult world—complicated rules and a history.

'They look happy,' Mma Ramotswe said.

Mma Potokwani smiled. 'They are very happy. No matter what they have had in their lives before, they are very happy.' She gestured for Mma Ramotswe to follow her into the office.

'I see you are driving a new van,' she said, as they sat down. 'It is very smart.'

Mma Ramotswe said nothing.

'And your old van? The white one?' asked Mma Potokwani.

'My old van has been retired. Mr J. L. B. Matekoni decided that he could not fix it any more.'

'He did that with our water pump,' said Mma Potokwani. 'I thought that it could go on a bit longer, but he said that it could not. They are like that sometimes—mechanics. They decide that the end has come and then nothing you say can make them think otherwise.' She paused. 'Are you sad, Mma? Sad about your van?'

Mma Ramotswe sighed. 'I am. But I think that I am going to get it back. I know where it has gone and I am going to go up there one day soon and find it. There is a man who has bought it to fix it up. I shall go up there—it's in Machaneng—and buy it back.'

She had not told anybody of this plan, had hardly determined it in her own mind, but now, rehearsed in this way before Mma Potokwani, it was the obvious thing to do. Yes, that was what would happen. She would go and find the tiny white van and bring it back. Mr J. L. B. Matekoni could hardly complain if she brought it back restored—it was not as if she would have to ask him to fix it.

'That sounds like a good idea,' said Mma Potokwani. 'Well done, Mma. It is a good thing to fight for the things you love.' She looked at her

230

guest. 'And that blue van out there,' she ventured. 'If you get your tiny white van back, then will you need that blue van? Because we're always looking for transport for the children, you see . . .'

Mma Ramotswe smiled ruefully. Mma Potokwani was incorrigible. But that would be too much. She could hardly give away a valuable van just because Mma Potokwani wanted it for the children.

'I'm sorry, Mma,' she said. 'I would love to give you that van, but it is worth quite a lot of money and Mr J. L. B. Matekoni . . .'

'Of course, Mma,' said Mma Potokwani. 'I understand. Now, let us talk about other things. We cannot sit here and talk about vans, like men do. We must talk about more important things.'

Mma Ramotswe took the initiative. 'Yes, we can leave that sort of talk to our husbands. That and football.'

Mma Potokwani laughed. 'Football! Yes, my husband is always going on about that with his friends. It is very dull for me.'

'Mind you, Mma,' said Mma Ramotswe. 'Some bits of football are quite interesting.' She looked down at the floor in modesty. 'As it happens, Mma, I have just solved a very major football case. Would you like to hear about it?'

It was why she had really come out to see Mma Potokwani, to tell her of the extraordinary resolution of the case of the Kalahari Swoopers. And it was an odd case, really—a very odd case. So she told her about her excursion into the world of football players and of the sudden, blinding insight that Puso had triggered.

'And was it the problem?' asked Mma

231

Potokwani.

'I think so,' said Mma Ramotswe. 'Of course I had a bit of difficulty persuading Mr Molofololo when I saw him earlier this morning. I told him that the reason he was losing was that the players all felt uncomfortable in the boots he was making them wear. He shouted at me, actually, and said that he had never heard such nonsense and that it was typical of the sort of idea that a woman would come up with. He was quite rude, actually, and I told him that I would not be spoken to like that and that he had better watch what he said. And do you know, Mma, that deflated him like a balloon. And he stopped shouting.'

'I would always listen to you, Mma,' said Mma Potokwani.

'Thank you, Mma. Well, he seemed to be thinking and after a while he telephoned the captain and started to talk to him about boots. The captain said much the same thing that I had said. And the captain also said, *Why don't you listen to anybody, Rra? Why don't you hear us when we try to talk to you?* Mr Molofololo started to shout about that, but I stopped him and said, *There you are, Rra—you are not listening, are you?* And he stopped. Just like that. He had heard something at last. After that he started to apologise to me. He said that he had learned a lesson and that he was very grateful for it.'

Mma Potokwani nodded approvingly. 'So what did you say then, Mma?'

'I said, *Here is my bill, Rra. It is ready for payment now.*'

'And?'

'And he paid. He paid very well, Mma. That is

why I have come out to see you, to tell you all about this and . . . and to tell you about another case. A very shocking one.'

Mma Potokwani listened open-mouthed as Mma Ramotswe told her the story of Violet Sephotho and her shocking attempt to ingratiate herself with Phuti Radiphuti. And when she came to tell her of the way in which Charlie had exposed the plan, the matron hooted with laughter. 'That boy really is quite a star,' she said. 'I have always said that. And yet he's still an apprentice.'

'He never does any work for his mechanical exams,' said Mma Ramotswe. 'He gets very bad results. It's his own fault.'

'He'll qualify one day,' said Mma Potokwani. 'Even if he doesn't get . . . what is the figure again, Mma?'

'Ninety-seven per cent,' answered Mma Ramotswe.

They both laughed. Then Mma Potokwani made tea, which she served with several slices of fruit cake. They drank three cups of tea each, and then, after a final slice of fruit cake—a small one—Mma Ramotswe got into her new blue van and drove back into town.

In the office, Mma Makutsi greeted her with the look that said, *You've missed something*.

'Somebody has been in, Mma Makutsi?'

'Yes. That woman.'

Mma Ramotswe looked blank.

'That Sephotho woman.'

She had not expected that. 'Violet?' Perhaps she had come in to threaten them; she would not put that past her.

'No, the other one. Lily Sephotho. The one with

233

two husbands.'

Mma Ramotswe sat down at her desk. It was turning into an eventful day, what with her successful resolution of the Molofololo case and now the return of the woman with two husbands.

'And what did she report, Mma?'

Mma Makutsi was evidently enjoying herself. 'She reported that she had done as we told her to. She had confessed to both husbands. And she said that both were very angry and threw her out. Our idea of choosing the one who was most forgiving was not a very good one. Neither was prepared to forgive.'

Mma Ramotswe spread her hands in a gesture of resignation. 'That really is her own fault, Mma. I'm sorry to say it, but it's her own fault. So what now?'

Mma Makutsi's enjoyment increased. 'Well, it gets better, Mma. She confessed to me that she hadn't really told us the whole truth. She hadn't told us that there was a third husband. She hadn't mentioned him because she was too embarrassed.'

'And this husband? What about him?'

'She says that she has learned her lesson, and she is keeping him. So she now has only one husband and everything has worked out well.'

'She is a very foolish woman,' said Mma Ramotswe. She stopped. Of course Lily Sephotho was foolish, but were we not all foolish, in one way or another, and did we not all deserve a second, or even a third chance?

Mma Ramotswe turned round. 'Well, I hope now that she is happy. Happier than her daughter at least . . .'

Mma Makutsi shook her head. 'No, she is not

Violet's mother, Mma Ramotswe. I asked her about that and she is an entirely different Sephotho. It is a coincidence that they both have names of flowers.'

Mma Ramotswe got to her feet. 'Well, Mma Makutsi,' she said. 'That settles all that. And everything else is settled, I think, which is how we really like it to be: settled. We are settled ladies, I think.' She glanced at the clock on the wall. 'So now we should get ready.'

'For what, Mma?'

'It is almost lunch time and I would like to treat you to lunch at the President Hotel.'

'The President Hotel!'

'Why not, Mma? We have earned a big fee from Mr Molofololo. We have sorted out at least one person called Sephotho, even if we have not sorted out the other one. And we are happy about all that, are we not?'

Mma Makutsi rose to her feet. She was wearing her new shoes, and she rather liked the idea of showing them off at the President Hotel. People appreciated shoes like that down there. 'We are, Mma. Yes, we are happy.'

'So let us go, Mma Makutsi, before all the tables are taken.'

They drove down to the centre of the town, parking the blue van at the back of the hotel. Then, as they were climbing the stairs at the front, Mma Ramotswe looked out, over to the east, and drew Mma Makutsi's attention to the clouds that had just appeared. They were distant purple clouds, and they meant rain, the longed-for rain that would start the growing season, would wake the land again.

'Look,' she said.

Mma Makutsi looked. 'Good,' she said.

There was nothing more to be said. It was good.

And at the table, in that silence as they contemplated the menu, Mma Makutsi's shoes suddenly addressed her. *Well, this is nice, we must say!*

Mma Ramotswe looked up from the menu. 'Did you say something, Mma?'

Mma Makutsi, who had been concentrating on choosing her lunch, had not been listening; after all, talkative shoes could not expect a constantly attentive audience. So she said nothing, but noticed, when she looked up, that the rain clouds had moved across the sky with great speed, and now they were not far away, over Mochudi perhaps, or near by, and the great veils of rain that dropped from those high clouds were now descending, like the traces of a giant brush across the canvas of the sky. And it was her turn to point and Mma Ramotswe's turn to look, and she said, 'That is the smell of rain, Mma.'

Mma Ramotswe said, 'Yes it is, Mma Makutsi. It is the smell of rain, the lovely smell of rain.'